D0571943

Open Arms

MYSTERY
and the
MINISTER'S
WIFE®

Open Arms

TRACI DEPREE

GUIDEPOSTS
NEW YORK, NEW YORK

Mystery and the Minister's Wife is a registered trademark of Guideposts.

Copyright © 2008 by Guideposts. All rights reserved.

The characters and events in this book are fictional, and any resemblance to actual persons or events is coincidental.

All Scripture quotations, unless otherwise noted, are taken from *The Holy Bible, New International Version*. Copyright © 1973, 1978, 1984 International Bible Society. Used by permission of Zondervan Bible Publishers.

www.guideposts.com
(800) 431-2344
Guideposts Books & Inspirational Media

Cover design by Dugan Design Group
Cover illustration by Rose Lowry, www.illustrations.com
Interior design by Cris Kossow
Typeset by Nancy Tardi
Printed in the United States of America

For Megan Rebecca

Chapter One

"Are you sure we're up for this?" Kate Hanlon asked as her husband, Paul, unlocked his office door.

She and Max Wilcox followed Paul into the dimly lit room. Paul flicked on the light.

The office was painted in a warm cocoa color. Lined with bookshelves and a large oak desk, it had a comfortable feel. Sunday-evening light floated in through the partially open blinds. Paul tugged a cardigan off a hook behind the door and slipped it on.

"Of course you're ready," Max said. "You're great with teenagers. I've seen how they take to you."

The curly-headed intern had been serving as Faith Briar's youth-group leader for the past several months, but he'd recently gotten a call to serve as a teacher at an orphanage in Guatemala, so they needed to replace him. Though they'd tried to find a suitable youth pastor or even a volunteer to take his place, no one had come forward.

"That wasn't there before," Paul said, pointing to his desk.

Kate followed his gaze to a pink envelope with a darker pink Hello Kitty cartoon stamped in the lower right-hand corner, and "To Pastor and Mrs. Hanlon" written in a loopy script across the front. He picked it up.

"That's really odd."

"What's inside?" Kate asked as her own curiosity rose.

Paul reached for a letter opener in the top drawer and neatly slit the envelope open. He scanned the page silently as Kate and Max looked on. His face fell.

Kate and Max leaned forward to get a peek at the letter.

"This girl sounds desperate," Paul whispered. He handed the stationery to Kate.

Dear Pastor and Mrs. Hanlon,

I don't know how to start this letter, so I'm just going to jump in. I don't have anyone else to turn to, but I've heard that you care about people, even people you don't know so well. So I thought maybe you could at least pray for me. I'm in so much trouble. My dad will spaz when he finds out. I'm afraid he'll kick me out of the house. But what can I do? Where can I go? It's not as if my mom's around for me to talk to.

Let me back up. The thing is, I'm pregnant. My boyfriend doesn't know. How can I tell him? Though he should know that he's going to be a father, shouldn't he? He's older than I am. I feel like I'm on shaky ground with him as it is. I just can't lose him. I'm afraid this will destroy everything between us. Everything is slipping through my fingers—my future, all my big plans once

I'm out on my own. I don't know how I'll be able to keep working and take care of a baby; it's not as if I make enough money to pay a babysitter. I'm too young for this. I don't know what to do.

I'm especially worried about my relationship with my father, which isn't too hot to begin with. I'm too afraid to tell anyone else, but I thought maybe you'd understand. I know that you really care. Please pray for me.

Yours truly,
Anonymouse

Kate noted the misspelling of the last word. As she lifted her eyes from the text, a sense of dread came over her. This poor girl! To be so alone and afraid . . . It was unfathomable. She handed the letter to Max, and her eyes met Paul's.

"Do you have any idea who it could be?" she said.

Paul shook his head. They waited for Max to finish reading.

"Wow," the youth leader whispered as he raised his head.

"Do you think it's someone in the youth group? Is there anyone who doesn't have a mother?" Kate asked him.

Max's eyes were wide. He scratched his stubbled chin and handed the letter back to Kate.

"Could be," Max said.

Paul handed the postmarked envelope to Kate. She studied the loopy script of the return address, which matched the writing in the letter. The *i* in "Mill" in Copper Mill had a heart where the dot should've been. On the lower left-hand

corner was a drawing, similar to a Celtic cross but more
ornate, with flowers and ladybugs coming out of it. It was a
doodle, but a really well-done doodle. Kate read the letter
again.

"This girl needs help," she said. She shook her head. "I
can't imagine how she must feel."

"Must be awful," Max said.

They made their way from Paul's office, down the stairs
off the foyer, and toward the fellowship hall as the noise of
teenagers arriving for youth group floated toward them.
Excited laughter bounced off the basement walls.

"I know the older girls pretty well," Max lowered his
voice. "Honestly, I can't picture any of them in this situation."
He paused as if to do a mental calculation. "Marlee Jones
seems to like the boys . . ." His words fell away. "I . . . there's
no way I could approach her . . ." He lifted his eyes to Kate's.

"It would be awkward to ask her something like that,"
Kate agreed, "and if it isn't her . . ."

"It could be anyone, after all." Max said.

"She may not even be in the youth group," Paul added. "It
could be a total stranger for all we know."

"What can we do?" Max looked between Kate and Paul,
his face furrowed with concern.

"You have enough to think about, with your new adven-
ture starting tomorrow," Kate reminded him.

Max laughed. "Oh, I forgot about that," he joked.

"We'll see what we can find out," Kate said. She glanced
at Paul, then added, "This is a plea for help if ever I saw one."

"And the girl was right," Paul said. "We *can* pray for her."

In the basement of Faith Briar Church, the three of them ducked into a vacant classroom. They bowed their heads in the darkness as they asked God for wisdom and comfort for a girl they didn't know.

THE BUZZ OF TEENAGERS swarmed around Kate and Paul. Their own children had been teenagers once, of course, but it had been a while since she and Paul had spent this kind of time with the energetic set. Youth group had been going on for an hour, and already she was exhausted.

Max stood at the front of the fellowship hall that served as the youth group's meeting place each Sunday night. With pale blue eyes and a mop of dark hair, he was a good-looking man in his early twenties. He held up his hands to settle the teens.

When the noise subsided, he winked at Kate and Paul.

"All right. As y'all know, I'm headed to Guatemala tomorrow morning . . ." He gazed around the room. "And we haven't yet found a replacement for me."

"I still can't believe you're deserting us," one of the boys in the front grumbled.

Max took a deep breath. "Guys, please understand. I've always wanted to do something like this, and when the opening to teach at the orphanage came up . . ."—he shrugged— "well, I knew it was an opportunity I couldn't pass up. That's how God is; he gives us open doors to walk through. If we didn't take them, who knows what great things we'd miss."

Max had an easy way with the youth that Kate appreciated. He'd come as an intern from a nearby Bible school a few months earlier and had shown himself to be the perfect man for the job. He had creative ideas that the teens were excited about, and a combination of energy and determination that kept him focused on finding the balance between meeting the students' social and spiritual needs. More and more Copper Mill teenagers had shown up for the Sunday-night meetings because of it.

One of the boys seated on the floor directly in front of Max raised his hand. Kate wasn't sure of his name. She glanced around the room at the others. Brenna Phillips and Marlee Jones sat silently next to each other at the back of the group of a dozen or so teens.

Kate had been watching all the girls to see if there was some way she could intuit if the sender of the letter was among them. Max had suggested Marlee. The typically exuberant teenager did seem a bit more reserved than normal, from what Kate could tell.

The Jenner boys were there—James and Justin, the sons of Kate and Paul's dear friends Livvy and Danny. James was sitting next to a pretty blonde named Anne Jackson, a new girlfriend, from what Livvy had told her. Kate hadn't seen Anne at youth group before, but she'd seen her around town. Perhaps she was someone to consider.

There was another new girl next to Anne with brown, silky hair and pale green eyes. She wore a light brown top with an intricate embroidered design that ran across the collarbone. Kate studied it for a moment—it had a Latin feel, like the cotton blouses she'd seen during a vacation to Mexico when she was a girl.

"So . . . ," the young man with the raised hand began,

drawing Kate's attention. "Who's going to lead the youth group while you're gone?"

Max cleared his throat. "Thanks for the segue, Brian." He grinned and motioned toward Kate and Paul, who were seated on metal folding chairs to the side of the group. "Pastor and Mrs. Hanlon have offered to take my place until they find another volunteer . . ."

Eyes shifted nervously to them. Kate felt their awkward stares and glued a smile on her face in an attempt to encourage them that it wouldn't be the end of the world.

Paul rose to his feet, ever the consummate pastor, and turned to face the group. He was a handsome man, at least Kate still thought so after almost thirty years of marriage. His brilliant blue eyes shone with a sparkle that said he was enjoying his new role.

"We'll need a lot of advice from you guys," he said. He gazed around the room as if taking in each face. "Any ideas you have for us to improve youth group, help you deepen your spiritual walks, and bring in new kids will be welcomed."

This time a girl raised her hand. Paul acknowledged her.

"Will we still have the afterprom party here?" she asked.

Paul looked to Kate, and she came to stand beside him. She had taken over the party that Max had planned to keep the high schoolers off the roads late at night while allowing them to continue the fun that would begin at the prom.

"Of course, we will," Kate assured. "I'll be heading up the committee in Max's stead, and I'll need as many of you to help make it as memorable as possible. Our next planning meeting will be Tuesday at five at the church. Even if you can't volunteer, you and your friends should still come to the party. It's a free event, and we already have a lot of great stuff planned—a photo booth that takes free pictures, a Velcro wall, and lots of other things still in the works. It's going to be a lot of fun."

The girl who'd asked the question sat back with a look of satisfaction, glanced at the friend next to her, and nodded. Apparently Kate had managed to appease them. At least for now.

Finally the meeting ended. The group got up and chattered, laughing loudly and roughhousing with one another. Many of the teens approached Max to hug him good-bye.

Marlee Jones was still in the back with Brenna Phillips. Kate glanced at her and noticed that her freckled cheeks were blotchy, and she kept her head down as if she didn't want anyone around her to see her face. Brenna placed an arm around her friend's shoulders. Kate went to talk to them.

"Did you hear that Marlee won the county art contest?" Brenna said when Kate came near. Marlee turned to wipe her tears.

"Really?" Kate said. "You don't look too happy about it."

"I'm okay," Marlee said with a shrug.

"She even won prize money," Brenna added, obviously proud of her friend.

"That's wonderful, Marlee," Kate said. "You like to draw?"

"I suppose."

It wasn't like Marlee to be so curt. Kate studied her for a long minute.

"Well, congratulations. I'd love to see the piece sometime."

"Mrs. Hanlon?" Anne Jackson came up.

Marlee and Brenna gave quick waves and meandered to

talk to someone else. Kate turned to Anne, who stood next to the brunette Kate had seen earlier. The girl smiled shyly, and Kate noticed the stud in the side of her nose.

"I'm so glad to see you here tonight, Anne," Kate said.

Anne smiled and said, "Thanks. I have a good time here. Everyone's so friendly." She glanced at the girl beside her. "I wanted to introduce you to Angie Petzel. She works with me at Emma's Ice Cream Shop."

"It's nice to meet you, Angie," Kate said, extending a hand to the tall, thin girl.

"Anne has told me a lot about you," Angie said, shaking Kate's hand.

"Good things, I hope," Kate laughed, and Angie nodded. "I'm glad you could come. What grade are you in at school?"

"I'm a senior."

"Do you have a home church?"

"Yeah, my family goes to a church in Pine Ridge, but their youth group . . ."—she shrugged—"it's not my favorite."

Kate patted her hand and said, "I hope you can come again."

"I'd like that." Angie smiled and nodded at Anne.

"We'll see you later, Mrs. Hanlon." Anne waved farewell.

As the teenagers left, chatting and carrying on, Kate paused. How would she figure out who had sent the letter? At least without offending some teenage girls and even their parents.

"Well, that went well," Max said, coming up alongside her.

"To quote Karen Carpenter," Kate said, "we've only just begun."

Chapter Two

Kim and Chad Lewis sat on opposite ends of the tan slip-covered couch in Paul and Kate's expansive living room. Chad crossed his arms tightly over his chest. His wife's gaze was glued to the floor. Kate and Paul were across the coffee table from them in matching overstuffed chairs.

Kate and Paul had met briefly with the couple two weeks earlier, and yet there seemed to be no difference in how they related to each other. Each blamed the other for their problems, and both hinted at separation. It broke Kate's heart.

Chad pushed his blond hair back from his forehead and leaned his forearms on his knees. He let out a heavy sigh.

"We aren't getting anywhere," he said, his blue eyes sagging in despair. "She hates me because we can't have kids. It's all I ever hear. I'm tired of the constant medical tests and the latest thing she saw on *Oprah* or *20/20* about infertility break-throughs and all the hocus-pocus this couple or that did to have a baby. I can't cope with it anymore. I want my life back."

Kim's face fell, and her eyes reflected sadness. "How can you say that? You're giving up on our marriage?"

Tears flooded her brown eyes as she turned them to Kate. "What am I supposed to do? He's rarely home lately"— she began the litany that had been the previous meeting's sticking points—"and he *said* he wanted children when we first got married."

"I *do* want children! But it's not happening. Can you—"

Paul held up a hand to stop him.

They were so young, in their late twenties. They'd been married all of six years, right out of college. In the past two weeks of counseling, Kate and Paul had learned that the Lewises had a seemingly perfect life until they'd started trying to have children. Then one year passed into the next, and still their cradle remained empty.

"This isn't about whether or not you can have children," Paul said, directing his gaze to Chad. "This is about your commitment to each other."

"But what if our love for each other is gone?" Chad said.

Kate shot a glance at Kim, who was visibly wounded by his words.

"*True* love starts when the feelings dim," Paul said. "I know that's not what popular culture says, at least not what we see on TV, but it's the truth. Love is a commitment first, to God and to each other . . . something we have to work on every day."

Kate's admiration for her husband grew each time he spoke of the commitment of marriage. They'd counseled many couples through their years in ministry, and in every session, Kate had been struck anew with the wisdom her husband held inside of him.

"I know you didn't come for counseling because you were ready to quit," Paul went on.

Kim and Chad's gazes met tentatively.

"You came here because deep inside you believe there's a solution, that you two can come together again. That your love can grow instead of die. Is that right?"

Kim turned to Chad, a vague hopeful expression in her eyes.

Paul smiled kindly. "We kind of danced around it last time. After giving it more thought, what do you think is the core of the problem?" He turned to Kim.

There was a long silence while she thought. She chewed her lower lip, and her brown eyes crinkled. Kim and Chad had only been attending Faith Briar for a few short months, since moving to Copper Mill from Chattanooga. She was a kindergarten teacher, and Chad was a CPA with a promising tax-accounting business in Pine Ridge.

"We came to Copper Mill for a fresh start," Kim began. She stared at her hands, which were folded in her lap. "Chad's parents are both deceased, and mine had just left for Indonesia to be missionaries. We wanted to be in a small town that felt close, like family . . . We're both only children, and I've wanted to be a mother for as long as I can remember." She smiled at a memory, then said, "During my growing-up years, I used to gather all the little kids in my neighborhood to play school. If their parents didn't know where they were, odds were I had them in my tree fort coloring or learning their ABCs. I was *meant* to be a mother. That's a big part of why I became a kindergarten teacher . . . my love of children."

Her eyes moved to her husband's, the pain-filled look in them unmistakable.

"I think a big part of our problem is just the stress of medical tests and miscarriages. So many disappointments. The doctors tell us there's no medical reason we can't have kids, but still . . ." She shrugged as unshed tears glistened in her eyes.

"But she blames me," Chad said under his breath.

"I do not," Kim said. "He thinks I do, but the truth is, he blames himself. No matter how much I tell him it isn't his fault. He stays late at work so he doesn't have to talk to me."

"You've filled your life with plenty of activities," Chad accused. "It's not like you're there even if I did come home."

"What am I supposed to do? Sit and wait? Even when you are home, you don't talk to me. You go into the bedroom and watch TV."

The volume of the conversation had risen considerably. Tension crackled in the air.

Kate set her coffee cup on the table and said simply, "You two need some ground rules."

Both of them gave Kate confused looks.

"When Paul and I first got married," Kate began, careful to keep any accusation out of her tone, "we laid down ground rules for arguing. They keep you from fighting dirty. When you start accusing and name calling, it's not constructive. For example, rule number one is 'always show respect.' That means listening with an open ear, being willing to really hear even those things we don't want to hear. None of us always says what we mean, so we need to learn to probe and find the intent behind the words." She paused and looked over to Paul, who was nodding his agreement, then she turned back to the couple. "You'll have to come up with your own rules, of course."

"That's a good point," Paul interjected. "And maybe we'll

make that part of your homework for next week. I want you to sit down together and come up with five rules for arguing, as well as some spiritual ground rules, that you both agree on. Like praying for each other every day. Once you agree, then you should commit to abide by them. It might even be a good idea to post them on the fridge."

"Do you have any suggestions?" Kim asked.

"Well," Kate began, then paused in realization. "We don't argue as much as we did when we were first married . . ."

Truth was, Kate couldn't remember the last time she and Paul had gotten into an all-out argument. They'd found such a natural way of living together that the very concept felt foreign. Of course, they still had their disagreements—all couples did—but they'd learned to understand each other even in the midst of them.

"Aside from 'always show respect,' another one of our ground rules for arguing is 'no changing subjects.' Changing the subject is a defense mechanism to point the finger back at your partner, but it defeats coming to a resolution.

"Another one is 'no leaving.' Leaving is dramatic, and it makes a big point when someone gets in the car and takes off, even if for a short time. But once you allow yourself to leave, it just gets easier and more tempting to go for good."

Kim and Chad exchanged guilty looks, and Kate suspected she'd touched a nerve.

"That's just a few, but you get the idea," Paul said. "Once you establish ground rules and respect your marriage enough to abide by them, you'll be on the right track."

Chad and Kim exchanged glances. Fear mixed with hope, Kate thought.

"You're on unsteady ground right now," Paul went on, "regardless of whether you can have kids. Besides, kids won't hold a marriage together—trust me. It gets harder once the children come. But you made a vow to God and to each other. Right now you *need* each other. Learning to come together during the hard times, not just the easy ones—that's what marriage is all about." He sat back in his chair and folded his arms. "So, tell me why you got married in the first place. What attracted you to each other?" He glanced from one to the other. "Kim?"

Kim fiddled with her wedding ring as she thought, then she smiled. "Well, I—"

"Don't tell me," Paul interrupted and motioned toward Chad. "Tell your husband."

A blush overtook her face as she turned. "I fell in love with you. That's why I married you. Because I like to spend time with you. You're funny and smart. You spoil me . . ." Her words fell away.

"Remember how I used to take you to the Chattanooga Choo Choo?" Chad said, then let out a soft laugh. "Those were good times."

"We were . . . a couple." Kim lifted her eyes to Chad's.

Kate noted his watery gaze. He straightened his back and moistened his lips with his tongue.

"I do love you," he said. His eyes flicked to Paul and Kate, then he went on. "I miss the walks we used to take, visiting that railway museum or just walking around Chattanooga."

Kim laughed. "By walking, you mean *hiking*. Eighteen miles in a single day." Then she sobered. "I miss that too."

"I married you because I want to spend my life with you,"

Chad went on. "You're a good cook. You're beautiful. You laugh at my jokes . . ." He sighed heavily. Then his gaze turned to Paul.

"We're already making progress," Paul said. "But this is just a first step. The negative habits you've established over these past few years need to be broken. I'd like each of you to take five minutes every day and tell your partner what you appreciate about him or her. You need to develop an attitude of gratefulness for your spouse."

Kim and Chad both nodded that they would do as instructed. Paul turned to Kate. "Is there anything you'd like to add?"

Kate shook her head.

"All right, then," Paul went on, rising to his feet. "We'll see you next Monday. In the meantime, work on those ground rules we talked about."

He shook hands with Chad, and they moved to the door.

"Thank you," Kim said, a tentative smile on her lips as she turned to Kate. "I feel like we made progress today. It's been a long time since I've felt that way."

The young couple left, and Kate slipped her arm around Paul's waist as they returned to the living room.

"Did I ever tell you that I love you?" she said.

"I think you mentioned it once or twice." He smiled and kissed her forehead.

KATE THOUGHT ABOUT the young couple all the rest of the evening, as well as the girl who'd sent the letter to Paul. There were so many disappointments in life. So many turns in the road that seemed impossible to maneuver at the time.

Her own life had had its hardships, yet God had brought her through, and he'd made her a better person because of them.

The letter with the loopy script lay on her nightstand. Kate picked it up and brought it to bed, turning on the light next to her. Paul was working in his study. She read the desperate words one more time. Her heart ached for this girl, and for Chad and Kim Lewis.

Paul's words echoed. *True love starts when the feelings dim.* And yet she'd found that on the other side of those hard times and passionless phases, there had been a deeper sense of love between them. Feelings always returned, fickle suitors that they were, stronger and more resonant. She loved Paul after all the years they'd been together, and she hoped Chad and Kim would someday know the kind of deep connection those decades together had brought to her own marriage.

A prayer welled up inside of her. "Lord," she began. "You've given me people to care for, to guide and help. There are two situations I know you're well aware of. The Lewises need wisdom and courage to make their marriage strong. Encourage them." She fingered the letter in her hand, the pink stationery so clearly that of a girl, not a woman ready to face the challenges of motherhood. "I don't know who wrote this letter. But you do. You know her and you love her. Help me to find her. She needs someone in her life who cares, who won't judge her . . . Someone who will show her what forgiveness is all about. Please stay near her, Lord."

As she ended the prayer, one thought remained: She had to find this girl. She had to reassure her that everything could be okay even if life itself seemed ready to tear her apart.

Paul came in from the study, kicking off his slippers into his side of the closet. He turned, and his eyes landed on the letter still in Kate's hands.

"Thinking about the girl?" he said.

Kate nodded. "And praying. I need to find her, Paul." She held up the letter.

Paul sat on the edge of the bed and smiled into her eyes. "I wondered how long it would be before you'd make this mystery your own."

Chapter Three

Kate had been cleaning all morning. She'd emptied out the refrigerator of its older residents and wiped the shelves and the condiment bottles. She'd swept and mopped the kitchen floor. She'd cleaned her teapot collection, which had gathered dust since her last tea party. Finally she moved to the living room, where she dusted and vacuumed, then swept the slate entryway.

Her thoughts were far from her tasks; instead, they focused on how to go about finding the stranger who'd mailed the letter. Paul had been surprised to find it on his desk so late on a Sunday . . .

She returned to the kitchen and called Millie Lovelace, the church's secretary.

The phone rang three times before Millie answered, "Faith Briar Church."

Kate pictured her tight gray curls and the way her face wrinkled in that irritated way when the phone pulled her away from whatever task she'd been doing. She was a gruff woman who had come with the church when Paul had taken over the pastorate. Her voice was scratchy, like someone who'd puffed on cigarettes for a lifetime, though she swore it was her husband and sons who partook of the habit and not her.

"Good morning, Millie, this is Kate."

"What can I do you for, Kate?" She sniffed.

"I'm wondering if you can help me with something."

"Depends," she said. "What do you have in mind?"

"Paul got a letter on Sunday. It was in a pink envelope with a Hello Kitty stamp in the lower left-hand corner. Do you remember seeing it?"

"You know, Pastor Hanlon already asked me about this."

"He did?"

"And I'll tell you the same thing I told him: it was just a regular letter. Came with Friday's mail, but since I had to leave for my job in Pine Ridge, I didn't get to sort it until Sunday. It's not like it's a big mystery or anything—just a letter in the mail. I couldn't tell you who it was from . . . Just another letter as far as I'm concerned."

"Oh." Kate sighed.

"You don't have to sound like your cat just died." Millie said in her unapologetic way. "What was in the letter anyway?"

"Millie," Kate interrupted as a thought came to her. "You've been around Faith Briar longer than I have. Tell me what you know about Marlee Jones."

"Marlee Jones? That little girl with the braces? Nothing really."

"What about her family? Do you know anything about her parents?"

"No. I've seen her father around town, I guess. Why do you want to know about them anyway? Was the letter from her?"

"No . . . I mean, I'm just curious about her."

"They don't come to church. I don't think they go to any church. But like I said, I don't really know."

"Would you say her father is judgmental?" Kate recalled the girl's fear of his reaction to her news.

"Don't all daughters think their fathers are judgmental?"

Kate thought about the comment. She supposed that any father who learned that his daughter was pregnant out of wedlock would be upset.

"I appreciate your talking to me," Kate said.

"Didn't have much of a choice. It's my job to answer the phone."

Kate smiled to herself as she hung up. The woman had a way about her, that was for sure.

She returned to the bedroom for the letter, then laid it out on the kitchen table alongside a yellow legal pad and began a bullet list of clues with the heading "Anonymouse," spelling the word the way the girl had in her letter. Was it a Freudian slip? Did she consider herself a mouse in a corner somewhere? Unnoticed, just scurrying about in her life with no one to turn to?

The first point Kate listed was "Pregnant." While it was a given considering the content of the letter, the clue offered a plethora of symptoms that Kate could base her evaluation on. She guessed the girl was in the morning-sickness phase of her pregnancy or would be soon, since no one else knew of her condition. She was bound to experience weight gain and moodiness, which typically accompanied the hormonal changes of pregnancy, not to mention sleepiness. With each of Kate's three pregnancies, she'd been unbelievably sleepy during the first few months, often going to bed just after supper and sleeping clean through to morning. Of course, pregnancies were as individual as people.

The second clue on her list was "Father issues." The girl was afraid of telling her dad the difficult news. Who could blame her? Even the best of fathers would have a hard time hearing such tidings. But there seemed to be more to this aspect than regular trepidation. And the girl had finished the letter by mentioning her father again.

Kate wondered if the girl even had a mother. She'd said, "It's not as if my mom's around for me to talk to." Kate made a special note to ask around town if there were any families who'd lost their mother or were divorced. Perhaps Livvy would remember any such families.

She lifted the envelope and noted the postmark. The letter was indeed sent from Copper Mill. That didn't prove the sender was a resident, but Kate felt it was a pretty strong indicator. Kate wrote the third point: "Probably a Copper Mill resident."

She studied the page again and wrote her fourth bullet point: "Boyfriend is older; doesn't know about baby." *But how much older is he?* Kate thought. Significantly? Or was he merely a year or two ahead of her in school, or just a few months older? She made a note to ask around about any May–December romances floating through the rumor mill.

Then she wrote her fifth and sixth points: "Works, but not enough to pay for baby" and "Has big plans once she's on her own." Her fear of being kicked out implied that she was still living at home.

Who is she? Kate tapped the pen against her chin. The pool of candidates in a town of thirty-five hundred was simply too big to narrow down.

Then realizing she'd forgotten another point she added, "Faith Briar member?" The letter hadn't said anything about where or if the girl went to church; she'd only said she heard that Paul and Kate cared about people. That would seem to indicate that the girl wasn't a Faith Briar attendee. Yet when Kate looked back through the letter, she noticed the sentence that read, "I know that you really care," which seemed to support the supposition that she was at least familiar with the church.

Kate lifted her face to the ceiling. She couldn't think of any young women who matched these clues. Frustration bubbled.

Just then, the front door opened. Kate could hear Paul taking off his spring jacket and hanging it on the coat tree.

"Katie? Where are you?" he called.

"In the kitchen," Kate said, realizing she hadn't started making lunch.

Being a pastor at a church just down the road meant that Paul could stop home in the middle of the day.

He came around the corner, a smile on his handsome face. "Say, do we have any plans tonight? I was thinking of going fishing with Sam and Danny later today. I've been invited to meet them at Danny's after he's done teaching for the day." He gave her a beguiling grin and lifted his eyebrows.

Sam Gorman, the church organist, owned the local

Mercantile, and Danny Jenner was a teacher at the Copper Mill High School.

"That's fine with me, but isn't it a little chilly out for fishing?" She moved to the refrigerator and pulled out cold cuts, lettuce, onions, and mayonnaise, then reached for the fresh loaf of whole-wheat bread in the cupboard and began to make sandwiches.

"Nah, it's fine," Paul said. "We're not planning on getting wet, just casting our lines out over Copper Mill Creek."

Kate shook her head, then broke into a grin.

"You're always into something, you know that?" She tugged him close by the front of his shirt.

"And that's a problem?" He smiled down at her as he wrapped his arms around her shoulders.

Kate lifted up on her toes and kissed his cheek. "Not a problem at all." Then she released him and turned to go. "I need to run into town to see Livvy and do some errands. Need anything?"

"Could you pick up some night crawlers and leeches? I do have to get back to the church this afternoon, so if you could get those, that'd be great."

"Night crawlers and leeches? Not on your life!" Even the thought of the creepy-crawlies made her shudder.

Paul's chuckle turned to a laugh. "Never mind, then. I'll pick them up myself when I head to Danny's. The guys will be there at three thirty." He glanced at his watch as Kate finished preparing his sandwich. "I better gather my supplies so I can grab my stuff and go right after work." He disappeared toward the general vicinity of the garage.

Kate ate her own sandwich, then picked up her list of clues and the letter, and tucked them into her handbag before heading to the garage. She waved good-bye to Paul and climbed into her black Honda Accord to head to town.

A chilly yet lovely spring day had descended on the quaint Tennessee valley. Sunlight touched the greening trees that arched over Smoky Mountain Road, and the morning mist had long since evaporated from the roadway. Ahead, Copper Mill shone like a jewel in the early afternoon sun. Steeples peeked from above the treetops, and the silver water tower reflected the light in a flash when it was at just the right angle. Kate squinted, wishing she'd thought to put on her sunglasses before she'd left the house.

Kate drove past Copper Mill Park, where toddlers were swinging and mothers chatted with one another on park benches. After taking a right onto Main Street, Kate drove past the Mercantile and pulled into the library's parking lot. In the heart of downtown, the Copper Mill Public Library was housed in a historic two-story brick building with green trim. There were several cars parked outside, including Livvy's SUV.

Kate gathered the books she needed to return and made her way inside the building. Patrons sat at the library's reading tables. Livvy's auburn head was bent over a computer at the main checkout station. She was engrossed in something on the screen, and she adjusted her glasses. When Kate set down her return items on the counter, Livvy looked up.

"Good afternoon, friend," she said. A smile touched her lips.

Kate returned the greeting as Livvy reached for the books and began to check them in.

"Say . . . ," Kate began, "I was wondering if you could help me with something."

Livvy raised an eyebrow. "Uh-oh. What's up now?"

Kate reached inside her handbag for the letter. "Paul found this on his desk last Sunday." She handed it to Livvy, then glanced around the quiet library. No one seemed to take note of them; heads were buried in books and magazines.

Livvy sent her a curious glance, then pulled the stationery from the matching pink envelope. Kate watched her face as she read. Livvy's brows knit together, and then her eyes filled with concern. When she lifted her gaze to Kate's, she was shaking her head.

"How sad," she said. "Do you know who it is?"

"That's the problem; I have no idea. It could be one of the girls from Faith Briar, but I'm not sure . . ."

She retrieved the bulleted list she'd made and laid that on the counter between them. "This is a list of the clues I have already. I was hoping you might be able to help me narrow it down since you work at the library and know more people in town than I do."

Livvy smirked slightly. "Another mystery?"

Kate shrugged. "You know me."

Livvy studied the list. "You spelled *anonymous* wrong," she said.

Kate pointed to the signature on the letter. "That's how she spelled it. I thought perhaps it was significant. And look at the drawing in the lower corner. It's quite impressive."

Livvy stared at the elaborate Celtic cross. "It's very detailed." She leaned back, her expression thoughtful. "So, what are you thinking?"

"First, I'm wondering if there are any widowers in town who have a teenage daughter. I guess I'm assuming she's a teenager, but she could be older. The only mention of a mother is here." She pointed. "I get the impression that the mother has either left or passed away. Actually," she continued, "I was thinking we should call Malcolm Dekker at the funeral home and ask if he knows of any teenage girls from Copper Mill who've lost their mothers."

Livvy nodded. "That's a great idea. Let's go into my office."

She turned and spoke to Morty Robertson, an elderly gentleman who volunteered once or twice a week at the library, asking him to man the station for her. He lifted his wrinkled face to Kate and gave her a wink. Livvy led Kate into her office.

"I've heard that Malcolm has a memory like a steel trap," she said as she pulled the phone book from her desk drawer and handed the telephone to Kate.

As a pastor's wife in San Antonio, Kate had attended more funerals than she could remember, so she'd come to know all the local funeral directors. But since she came to Copper Mill, there had only been a handful of funerals to speak of. Even still, she'd become acquainted with the odd little man who was Copper Mill's only funeral director. She had found him both eccentric and pragmatic—a combination she hadn't known was possible until she met him.

A winded voice came on the line just as Kate was about

to hang up. "Dekker Funeral Home," Malcolm Dekker said in his whiny voice.

"Malcolm," Kate said, "this is Kate Hanlon. How are you today?"

"Sorry, I don't have time to chat. Did someone die?"

"No . . ."

"I've gotta run, then. I'm in the middle of something."

"Oh, I'm sorry. Is there a better time to call? I need to ask you some questions."

He sighed, and then there was a long moment of silence.

Finally he said, "My meeting should be done in forty-five minutes. Why don't you just stop by? I hate talking on the phone."

"Oh. All right. I'll be there then." She hung up.

"Well?" Livvy said.

"He couldn't talk. I'm going to stop by after I finish some errands. So . . ."—Kate turned her attention back to the list— "I noted that the girl's boyfriend is older than she is. But the letter didn't say by how much, and she seems really insecure about their relationship. Do you know of any romances in town where the boy is older than the girl?"

Kate sat back and studied her friend's hazel eyes as she considered Kate's question. "Hmm . . ." Livvy chewed on her lower lip. "There was Mabel Trout's daughter and that film producer."

"Really?" Kate leaned forward in her chair.

"But I think he died a couple years ago . . ."

"That doesn't really fit then."

Livvy finally shrugged her shoulders. "I can't think of anyone.

Besides, I don't know enough teenage girls to have any idea. That's the problem with having sons; I only get to know the boys. Unless one of my boys brings a girlfriend home, of course."

"I saw James's new girlfriend at youth group."

Livvy smiled. "Anne. She's a nice girl."

"How long have they been going out?"

"A couple of months. You know how these things are. One day they're on, the next they're off." Livvy laughed.

Kate nodded, remembering all too well the influx of girl-friends and boyfriends her son and daughters had brought through their home when they were younger.

Finally Kate returned to the topic at hand, pointing to the list. "Do you think Justin and James would know of any such relationships, especially if she isn't living with her mother?" Kate asked.

"I'll ask them after school. Wait, the afterprom meeting is tonight, right? They'll both be there."

"I can ask them then," Kate said, then paused. "But I don't want to start any rumors around school by asking too many questions either."

"You're right. That could be a problem. I'll ask when they get home tonight," Livvy said. "Kids expect their mothers to be nosy."

Kate glanced at her watch. "Which reminds me . . . I'd better get a move on. What time are the men coming home from fishing tonight? Paul didn't mention where he was eating."

"The men are going fishing?"

"Danny didn't tell you?"

Livvy shook her head. "Men" was all she said. Then she and Kate stood.

"Can I photocopy those?" Livvy asked, pointing at the letter and the bulleted list.

"Of course." Kate handed the papers to her friend.

"I'll noodle on the clues. Maybe something will come to me."

After Livvy photocopied the pages and returned them, Kate left to run her errands before heading to the funeral home. She stopped at the post office to purchase a roll of stamps and at the gas station, where she filled up her tank.

She was on her way to the funeral home when she noticed Emma's Ice Cream, an old-fashioned ice-cream shop and candy store in downtown Copper Mill. Remembering that Anne Jackson and Angie Petzel, whom she had met at youth group, worked there, she stopped in for a treat.

Emma, the owner and namesake of the place, was stocking bins of candy that lined one wall, and Angie was working the cash register. Angie glanced up as Kate stepped in front of the ice-cream freezer and gazed through the glass, trying to decide what flavor she was in the mood for. They had the regulars like vanilla and Rocky Road, chocolate and mint chocolate chip, as well as their house specials that Emma perfected herself, flavors like "Walloping Watermelon" and "Peanut Butter Melt-Away."

Angie came over. "Hey, Mrs. Hanlon. Can I help you?"

Kate smiled at the girl. Her high cheekbones gave her face angular lines, and she had striking pale green eyes. She wore a cute multilayered outfit—a tank with lace that peeked from beneath a lime-green tank, and a lightweight yellow sweater with intricate embroidery along its neckline. A scarf like a headband covered her silky brown hair, and she had a different post in the side of her nose—this time a simple gold dot that looked like a ball bearing.

"Do you have any recommendations?" Kate asked, tempted by several flavors.

Angie studied the selections for a moment. "Depends on your taste. I'm not one for the real sugary stuff."

Kate found the statement ironic, considering the girl worked in an ice-cream parlor. When she glanced up, she saw a note by the register that read, *Marlee out sick today.*

"Oh, Marlee works here?" Kate asked.

Angie nodded. "Emma just hired both of us since Brenna Phillips hasn't been able to put in as many hours during the school year."

Kate glanced at her watch, realizing school was still in session. "I thought you were still in school . . . ," she said.

"Yeah, I'm a senior. I get to leave campus during free periods so I can work here."

"Sounds perfect." Kate found her eyes lingering on the girl's nose ring. Finally she said, "That's . . . cute." She pointed to the same spot on her own nose.

Angie lightly touched the gold post. "Thanks." She gave an awkward laugh and then straightened her tall frame slightly. "So . . . ?" She directed Kate's attention back to the ice cream.

"Oh," Kate said, quickly making her choice. "I'll take the mint chocolate chip."

"Sugar cone or cake?"

Kate pointed to the sugar cone, and Angie began scooping the ice cream.

Kate studied the girl, her mind floating back to her quest. Could Angie be the one? She seemed like a confident, put-together young woman. She had healthy color in her cheeks, and she was thin, with a flat stomach. Whoever the anonymous girl was, she might be exhibiting some outward signs of her pregnancy by this time, and the fact that Angie was so confident seemed incongruent with the devastated, frantic nature of the letter.

Kate's gaze returned to the note by the register. Marlee was out sick. Kate took note.

She thanked Angie, then moved to the wall of bins, where Emma was working away. At Kate's greeting, the rotund woman lifted her sallow face, which lit into a smile.

"Kate, it's great to see you," Emma said. "You need some candy? Am I in your way?"

Kate smiled and said, "Actually, I was wondering if you have a minute to talk?"

Emma looked around the shop, then nodded to one of the empty tables near the front of the store, where no one would hear them.

They each took a seat, and Emma looked expectantly at Kate. "What's on your mind?"

"I . . ." Kate cleared her throat. Then she pursed her lips and started over. "I have some questions for you about . . . Marlee."

Emma leaned toward her until Kate could smell the mint on her breath. "You mean my employee, Marlee?"

Kate nodded.

"It isn't like you to gossip, Kate Hanlon," she said.

Kate smiled. "It's not my intent to gossip. Trust me."

"What is it you think she's done? She's only worked here a couple of weeks."

Kate nodded that she was aware of the fact. "I was just wondering what you know about her home life, her interests. Does she have a mother?"

"Oh." The expression on her face said she didn't understand why Kate would want to know about the girl. Nonetheless, she went on. "Well, Marlee is an only child. I don't know much about her parents. She's a pretty good worker, as far as teenagers go. She has been moody lately and has even missed work a couple times. She's out sick today."

"I saw the note," Kate said.

Emma's eyes widened. "So this has something to do with her health?"

Kate held up a hand to stop her. "I can't say what it's about. I'm sorry, Emma. But trust me; I have good intentions."

Still, Emma's brow furrowed.

"Let me ask you this. Has she seemed ill when she does come in?" Kate ventured.

"Like I said, she's only worked here a couple of weeks . . ." Emma shrugged.

She stood and thanked Emma for her time. The woman had a disappointed expression on her face, but Kate wasn't about to divulge any information. She returned to her car.

She didn't know Marlee very well yet, and the truth was, she wanted to develop a strong relationship with all the girls in the youth group. She couldn't just blurt out, "Are you pregnant?" After all, she'd just taken over the youth group. She still had trust to build with the group.

The letter hadn't said how far along the girl was, but Kate had deduced she was early in the pregnancy, because nobody knew about it yet. It would soon become all too evident. If only Kate had the wisdom of Solomon to figure out who the poor girl was before she had to face that humiliation alone.

Chapter Four

B y the time Kate got to Dekker Funeral Home on the south side of town, almost an hour had passed since their phone call. Kate hoped the man would be ready to talk.

She made her way up the stone walkway and through the double doors at the front of the one-story white building. It was a run-of-the-mill funeral home, at least on the outside, with its white facade and twin pillars that flanked the double-wide front doors. Yet inside was a memory of some bygone era. Faded maroon velvet curtains with gold tiebacks fringed with tiny pom-poms framed the windows from ceiling to floor. The carpet was a busy pattern in golds and browns, though the center was so worn that the backing showed through in spots. Floral wallpaper continued the busy theme and gave the place a boudoir feeling that seemed incongruent with the dignified nature of funeral homes.

"Hello?" Kate called.

There was no answer. Kate moved toward the office. It was deathly quiet.

"Hello?" Kate called again.

She walked to the back of the building. An open door revealed a large room with chairs lined up and an open casket at the front. Bouquets of flowers were arranged here and there. A woman was setting up an easel with a collage of photographs at the far side of the room.

"Excuse me," Kate said. The woman lifted her head. "Do you know where Malcolm is?"

"He's in the embalming room." The woman pointed behind Kate. "It's down those stairs, in the basement. First door on the left."

Kate thanked her and turned to go, but when she reached the stairs, Malcolm Dekker was coming up. The funeral director was a short, skinny man with Coke-bottle glasses and a receding hairline. His teeth were yellowed and stained, causing Kate to wonder if he'd ever set foot in a dental office. He lifted his gaze to Kate's and pushed his glasses up on his nose.

"You *are* here," he said, then motioned for Kate to follow as he led the way to his office. "I have a viewing in an hour, so we're going to have to make this snappy." He pointed toward the room where Kate had spoken with the woman and added, "Poor guy was in a freak accident at work. He was in construction."

Kate glanced toward the open casket. She could make out dark hair and a sallow-looking face beneath a spray of flowers that read "Dad" in the lid of the casket. Kate imagined the grieving family. To lose someone in the prime of life was more than a tragedy; it disrupted everything, put children in hard situations, left spouses devastated. Kate inhaled a deep

breath and was surprised to realize that even the death of a
stranger could choke her up.

When they reached the office, Kate took one of the
leather chairs opposite the large walnut desk where Malcolm
sat. As he leaned his elbows on the massive piece of furniture, he reminded Kate of a child in need of a booster seat.

The surface was empty save for a framed photograph and
a newspaper. The photograph was of a girl. Kate studied it for
a moment. She looked familiar, with bleached hair.

"On the phone you said you had a question . . ." Malcolm
interrupted her musing.

"Oh yes," Kate began. "I'm wondering if you know of any
widowers in town who might have a teenage daughter."

Malcolm raised his eyebrows and wiped his nose with
a handkerchief that he pulled from his suit pocket. "In the
market for a new family, are you?" the man said with an odd
little sniffle.

Kate couldn't tell whether he was serious. Then a grin
spread across his wrinkled face, and those yellow teeth drew
Kate's gaze.

"I'm just teasin' you, Missus Hanlon."

She smiled. "Actually, I'm looking for someone and
thought since you're the one who handles the funerals in
town, you might be able to recall any women who died and
left a husband with young or teenage children."

She glanced at the photo again, and then she realized who
it was. Arlene Jacobs. The young woman who worked as a
part-time cashier at Sam Gorman's Mercantile. The unfamil-
iar setting had thrown Kate off. She hadn't considered Arlene,

but the young woman was about the right age, was familiar
with Kate and Paul, and could have heard more about them
through Sam.

"Recent deaths?" The man stroked his leathery chin with
his forefinger and thumb.

"I'm not sure."

"Now, this is curious, Missus Hanlon. What are you digging for? Someone's long-lost relative? You're not giving me a
whole lot to go on."

"I don't have a whole lot to give you," Kate said. "They
would be residents of Copper Mill, I think. Are you related to
Arlene?" She pointed to the picture.

Malcolm ignored her question. "What's this for?" He
leaned forward, his gaze scrutinizing.

"It's personal," Kate said. Then realizing that the man
might choose not to help her, she added, "I got a letter from
the girl, and she's in trouble. It's imperative that I find her."

"Well..." The funeral director scratched his balding
head, then met Kate's direct gaze. "What does Arlene have to
do with it?"

"Oh, nothing. I was just surprised to see her picture."

"She's my niece," he said, his eyes narrowing. "The only
family I have." He paused to scratch his chin. "Anyway, I can
think of a couple people whose mothers died. But I don't
know if they still live in Copper Mill."

"That'd be great." Kate leaned forward in her chair. "Any
leads you can give me would be appreciated."

Malcolm stared at her. Just then the front door opened,
and the sound of voices and sniffling entered the foyer.

He glanced at his watch. "Oh, rats, the family's here already," he said. "Tell you what, I'll think about it and call you."

Kate thanked him and jotted down her phone number. Then she said farewell and left Malcolm, who had gotten out a comb and was meticulously straightening what hair he had in the mirror next to his door.

As Kate passed the grieving family—a mother with four young daughters—and saw their stricken, tear-streaked faces, she realized how very frail life could be. She sent up a prayer for them.

KATE WAS HOME BEFORE THREE O'CLOCK. She'd wanted to touch base with the coordinators Max had arranged for each area of the afterprom party and find out what had been accomplished so far. Hopefully it would save them all time at their meeting that evening. While Max had been a great youth leader, he hadn't been very organized in planning the party. Kate preferred to have things written down so her memory wouldn't have quite that heavy a burden.

Since Faith Briar Church was hosting the festivities, Max had recruited volunteers from among their own congregation. Some people had suggested allowing the teens to manage the event themselves, but with the huge amount of work required and the many commitments of high-school life, including the prom itself, that idea had quickly been dismissed.

Kate dialed Renee Lambert first. The feisty seventy-one-year-old answered on the fourth ring.

"Kate," she said. "I was going to call you."

"Oh?"

"Do you want me to bring something for the meeting tonight? A pie or something?"

"I've got it covered, Renee. But thanks anyway," Kate said. "LuAnne is bringing caramel rolls. I am calling about tonight, though. Max gave me a list of people he'd contacted to help with the afterprom party, but he didn't tell me what each person's job is or where we are in the process of getting things ready."

Renee laughed. "LuAnne and I are in charge of food. She's calling parents to donate cookies and cakes and that kind of thing, and I'm coordinating the hot food."

"Okay, that helps a lot." Kate jotted down the information. "Have you decided what food we're going to serve?"

"Some of that depends on the budget, so you might have to tell me. Either Sloppy Joes or pizzas."

"Perfect. I think that's all I need for now. We can discuss the details more tonight so everyone can add their input."

"Okeydoke." Renee hung up.

Then Kate called Carl Wilson. He and Joe Tucker were in charge of building the game booths for the event. Carl told her that he was still waiting for the go-ahead to get the lumber, and as soon as it arrived, he'd be on top of it. All they needed were adequate funds to pay for it all.

Betty Anderson and Livvy Jenner were handling the fundraising and publicity aspects of the event.

Since the party was a community-wide endeavor, the funds were coming in, Betty told Kate. They were planning a car wash in the near future and had sent out letters to all the families of the teenagers in town, asking for a twenty-dollar-a-head donation. People had already started sending in money.

When Kate was done making her calls, she glanced through her to-do list. One of the mothers had taken the task of finding out about game rentals and reporting back about those possibilities. Since Renee and LuAnne were in charge of the food, they would coordinate cooking, serving, and cleanup. But she would still need to find out about decorations, as well as line up the many volunteers they'd need that night to chaperone.

She ran a hand through her strawberry blonde hair and exhaled. What had she gotten herself into?

Paul buzzed in and out at three o'clock as he'd told her, and she popped some frozen lasagna in the microwave to eat before she headed to church later that afternoon to meet with the afterprom committee. She wasn't in the mood to cook for herself.

The theme of the afterprom party, Max had said, was "Under a Starry Sky," which coordinated with the "Evening in Paris" theme of the prom itself. Both lent themselves to soft lighting and romantic settings, though the committee had already communicated to the parents that their children would be well supervised during the event.

Just before she left for church, Kate called Livvy to check in.

"Hey," she said. "Did you think of anything new after I left?"

"No," Livvy said. "I'm still thinking about it though."

"What do you know about Marlee Jones?"

"Not much. I've seen her at church once or twice, but she only comes with Brenna Phillips. I really don't know her at all."

"She was the first person Max mentioned after he saw the letter," Kate said. "He said she was boy crazy. And whenever I've seen her, she's been outgoing and bubbly. But on Sunday, she was very aloof as if she didn't want to be there and I could see that she'd been crying."

"I'll see what I can find out about her," assured Livvy.

Kate thanked her and hung up and then drove the short distance to the church.

When she pulled into the church parking lot, several other cars were already there. Grabbing her planner and notebook from the front passenger's seat, she made her way inside. Joe Tucker was helping himself to a cup of coffee when Kate came into the downstairs kitchen.

"Hello, Kate," Joe said. The fluorescent lights reflected on his bald head. "Want some coffee?"

"Sounds great," Kate said, setting her handbag and planner on the counter.

Joe set down his own Styrofoam cup, then reached for another cup from the stack and pressed the coffee spigot on a large urn to fill it.

"So, how's it feel to be youth-group leader?" he asked.

He turned to hand her the steaming coffee, which she gratefully accepted.

"I've worked with the youth before in San Antonio, so I'm slowly reacclimating. I'd forgotten how much energy teen-agers have," Kate confessed.

Joe grinned and gazed around the fellowship hall, which was filling with volunteers.

"I gotta hand it to you, Kate," he said. "It's an intimidating task. Kids these days can be so hard to figure, with all their gadgetry. Parents spoil 'em much more than they did in our day."

"I don't know about that," Kate said, feeling his eyes fixed on her. She took another sip of her coffee. "Some kids are spoiled in every generation. It depends on the individual, doesn't it?" She turned to meet his eyes.

Joe's lips met in a thin line. "I s'pose," he finally said. "All I know is I don't envy your job."

"Don't get me wrong," Kate said with a laugh. "I miss Max already."

Joe chuckled and took a sip of his steaming brew.

She wished she could ask Max about the letter again. He knew the teens so much better than she did. But his plane had taken off the previous morning. He was probably meeting with children at the orphanage that very moment, discovering what life in a foreign country was like.

Just then, Anne Jackson and the Jenner boys came in, taking seats in the back of the fellowship hall. For a moment, Kate thought of the possibility that her dear friend's son could be the unsuspecting father, and her heart ached for what such news would mean for Livvy. Then she realized it didn't matter if it was her friend's son or someone else's. The pain would be no different.

"You okay, Kate?" Joe asked, drawing her attention back to the present.

She smiled at him and patted his hand.

"Sorry 'bout that. My mind does tend to wander as I get older."

"Ain't that the truth!" he agreed.

Kate snatched up her handbag and planner and led the way into the fellowship hall, where people were taking their seats at the long tables. Joe followed her.

Only a handful of teens were there. As much as she'd talked it up at youth group, Kate was disappointed that more of the students hadn't shown up. She wanted them there not to coordinate or plan the party but because she believed that if they got involved in even a small way, they'd see the many fun activities slated for the night and tell their friends.

So when Kate rose to start the meeting, she made sure to say, "Let's do what we can to get all the teens excited about this party, otherwise they won't come. We know from experience and statistics that parties like this help keep teens safe and protect them from making poor decisions because of peer pressure. Studies have shown that there are fewer highway deaths on prom nights since afterprom parties have become the norm. So let's get out there and ask for more volunteers. Let's do more advertising."

She looked to Livvy, who gave a rundown of the fundraising and publicity aspects of the party and what she was doing to get the word out. She'd lined up a series of ads on the local radio station, which, she added, had offered the slots for free as a public service. She was making posters to put up around town a couple of weeks before prom, as well as print ads that would run in the *Copper Mill Chronicle*.

Satisfied that Livvy had that aspect of the party under control, Kate glanced down at her notes.

"There's the car-wash fund-raiser coming up. When is that?" She looked at Livvy again, and Betty, who was seated next to her.

"It's next week," Livvy said. "We've decided to have it at the library. There's a hose hookup outside the building, and since it's downtown, we should be able to drum up some business."

Then Kate gestured toward Renee Lambert, who talked about the menu with her dog Kisses clutched under her arm.

"We're going to *buy* pizza, not make it?" LuAnne Matthews interrupted, a puzzled expression on her face. The Country Diner waitress was still wearing her polyester work uniform, minus the white apron. "It'd be cheaper to make it, or the Country Diner could cater, couldn't we?"

Renee made an impatient sound in the back of her throat as she looked from LuAnne to Kate. "Teens do *not* want Country Diner food! And if you want to go to all the work of making pizzas . . . I suppose we can do that. But it seems silly to me."

Kate raised a hand to halt the impending argument. "Let's do a cost comparison," Kate said. "Can you take care of that, Renee?"

Renee sniffed indignantly, then gave a reluctant nod.

ONCE THE MEETING HAD ADJOURNED, James Jenner came up to Kate. He was a stocky boy, with hazel eyes like his mother, and dark curly hair like his father.

Kate wondered if Livvy had had a chance to talk to him yet.

"What's on your mind, James?" Kate asked.

"I just wanted to let you know that some other kids were talking about helping out."

"Oh," she said. "That's good."

"Some of them were busy, so they couldn't make it tonight, and I'll see if I can recruit some kids from the baseball team too."

"That would be awesome, James." Kate patted his thick shoulder, and the boy smiled. It was a winsome smile, handsome, and Kate thought it wouldn't take a whole lot for a pretty girl like Anne Jackson to fall under its spell.

Chapter Five

A s Kate was pulling into her driveway at seven o'clock that evening, her cell phone buzzed to life. Digging in her handbag, she found the gadget and pushed the Talk button.

"Is this Kate Hanlon?" asked the whiny voice on the other end of the line.

Kate instantly recognized it as Malcolm Dekker's and hoped the funeral director had some information for her. Her thoughts flitted to Arlene Jacobs, the girl in the photo on his desk.

"Malcolm," Kate said. "How are you?"

"I don't have time for chitchat, but I wanted to let you know that I thought of a few people whose mothers died, leaving the father to raise the children alone. Mind you, it wasn't recent. Were you looking for something more recent?"

"Not necessarily," Kate said.

"Riley Waters lost his wife about two years ago. He had three teenage daughters."

"Really?" Kate straightened in her seat and reached for a pen in her handbag to write down the names.

"Then there were the Joneses on Sweetwater Street. Maridee was the mother. Do you know them? The dad was David. It was ten years ago. But the mother died in an accident at the old mill. It was a grizzly affair, had to have a closed casket. But they had one daughter—Marla or Marva, something like that."

Kate was stunned. Jones. Did he mean Marlee Jones's mother? By the time Kate was ready to confirm the name, Malcolm was saying, "Well, I have flowers at the door and a makeup job to start, so I'd better go." Then he clicked off.

Kate stared at the receiver and made her way into the house. Why hadn't she known that Marlee was motherless? Even Emma hadn't known. Wouldn't it have come up? But then it had been a long time since her mother had died. Perhaps Marlee assumed that everyone knew, or maybe it was so private and painful that she hadn't wanted to talk about it. Either way, the girl had masked a very deep hurt.

What other hurts had she hidden?

WHEN KATE CAME IN, she found Paul reclining in the living room, with soft music playing and a book in his lap. He lifted his head and gave a little wave, then went back to his story.

Kate pulled out the pink envelope from her purse and read through it again. Then she went into the bedroom to call Livvy at home. Livvy picked up on the first ring.

"Jenners'," she said.

"It's me again," Kate said. "I think it's possible that Marlee Jones's mother passed away."

"Really?"

"Malcolm told me that someone died ten years ago in an accident at the old mill, and it sounded like it could be her."

"That's horrible," Livvy said. "But I wonder if there are any stories about it in the archives."

"I was just thinking the same thing," Kate said. "I'll look up the obituary for David Jones's wife. Her name was Maridee."

"That sounds like a good place to start. Oh, by the way, I talked to the boys," Livvy went on. "They mentioned a few couples at school where the boy is older than the girl. Marlee Jones does have an older boyfriend, and so does Lauren Clark. Lauren's boyfriend is in Austria as a foreign-exchange student this year."

"*Hmm,*" Kate said, "he probably would've left at the beginning of the school year, right? That's almost seven months ago . . ."

"Good point."

"Justin mentioned that Marlee does a lot of posting on FriendsForever."

"What's FriendsForever?" Kate asked.

"It's one of those Internet social networks. All the kids have a page. My boys are on it most every day after their homework is done."

Kate didn't remember ever hearing of the site, which made her feel out of touch. Yet a Web site like FriendsForever might be very helpful in learning more about the girls in town. Her thoughts turned back to James.

"Um," Kate began, conscious that she was about to ask a delicate question. "What do you know about Anne Jackson?"

"Anne? Well . . . wait . . . what are you suggesting?" Livvy's tone became defensive immediately.

Kate suddenly felt sorry for mentioning it.

"I didn't mean any—" Kate tried to say, but Livvy wasn't finished.

"James is *not* that kind of boy, Kate."

"I know he's not. I'm sor—"

"You know, sometimes, Kate Hanlon, your sleuthing can go too far. You can't just go around town suspecting people. I can't even believe you would suggest such a thing." Then she hung up.

Kate stared at the receiver, which started beeping in her hands. What had she just done?

The reality of how very delicate this situation was came at her full force. Livvy was right. If she went around town asking teenage girls if they were pregnant, it would ruffle a lot of feathers, maybe even sever relationships. She closed her eyes as a wave of sadness fell on her, then she placed the receiver back in its cradle.

She felt awful. Should she call Livvy back? She covered her face with her hands.

AN HOUR LATER, Kate could stand it no longer. She picked up the phone and dialed the Jenners' number. Someone picked up the receiver, and Kate said, "Livvy?" before the person could speak.

She heard a sigh and a sniffle.

"I'm sorry," Kate said.

"I'm sorry I reacted so strongly," Livvy said in a quiet voice. "I've been sitting here feeling just awful."

"I should've thought before I spoke. I know that James is a good guy. It was wrong of me to assume otherwise—"

"No," Livvy interrupted. "That's where I was wrong."

"What do you mean?"

"It was judgmental of me to think that my children are above something like that. Everyone has weaknesses. My boys could very well make those choices too—and nobody is beyond forgiveness."

Kate smiled at her friend's words, thankful that she could still call her friend.

"I actually asked James about it when I got off the phone," Livvy said.

"You didn't."

"Not in so many words. I asked him if he and Anne have been tempted . . . He was mortified at first, but then he told me he wouldn't do anything like that. He knows how important it is to respect her and to respect his future wife."

Relief flooded over Kate. "That's good news."

"I also asked for suggestions about how to understand what kids these days care about. He suggested you open a FriendsForever account to connect with the kids in the youth group."

"When you mentioned it before, I wondered the same thing," Kate said, not sure she felt comfortable with the idea of joining such a group. How would the kids react to having an old lady in their "space"? And how much would they be willing to share with her?

"I monitor our boys' online activity pretty closely on that site, and it all seems pretty clean. I mean, they are still teenagers, so you have to take some of the things they say with a grain of salt. But nowadays, it's how kids keep in touch with each other. They're constantly chatting online. They always know what's going on with each other. Hey, even Barbara Walters has a MySpace account. That's a similar site."

"Could you help me set it up?"

While Kate fared pretty well on the Internet, she knew her limits, and Livvy was a pro at such things.

"Stop by the library tomorrow morning. I'll be happy to help."

Chapter Six

The library had been open for half an hour when Kate came in the next morning. Not a single patron was there except Kate. Livvy was nowhere in sight. Kate stood in front of the horseshoe-shaped counter near the front door and glanced at Livvy's office. A placard on the door read "Olivia Jenner" and below that were the words "Head Librarian."

Kate poked her head through the doorway to see if Livvy was sitting at her desk, but she wasn't there either. Deciding that she must be upstairs at the high-speed computers, Kate climbed the stairs to the second floor.

Sure enough, Kate found Livvy staring at a monitor. She glanced at Kate and offered a smile of greeting. Kate was warmed by the gesture. Livvy patted the second chair she'd pulled up alongside her.

"I thought I'd get a head start on this," Livvy said. "I have a toddler reading hour in half an hour."

Kate nodded and gazed at the screen, where her name, e-mail address, and home address had already been filled out. Livvy hit Submit and waited.

"You've got it all set up," Kate said, impressed.

"Actually, you need to go into your e-mail account and click on the link they just sent you that ensures you are who you said you were."

Kate did as she was instructed, and soon had the site back on the screen. Livvy hit another button to upload a photo of Kate to the profile.

"Where did you get the picture?" She leaned in to examine it more closely. It was a close-up of her at the diner, a cup of steaming tea in her hands.

"I have my ways," Livvy said with a raised eyebrow. "There's still a lot to do." She pointed to the screen. "You need to complete your profile and build a network of friends. See, here is where you can invite people to join your FriendsForever circle." She clicked around the screen, showing Kate the many features of the site, including photographs, private e-mail, and a bulletin board where people could type public messages to one another.

Before long, Livvy excused herself to get back to work, and Kate invited kids from the youth group as well as any others she could think of to be her "friends." Once they accepted her invitation, she would be able to chat with them about their day, see their photographs, and post messages.

Brenna Phillips must have been in a computer lab at the high-school library because she accepted the invitation minutes after Kate sent it. She posted "Great to see you here, Mrs. Hanlon" on Kate's bulletin board.

Kate typed, "What are you up to?" and hit Send.

Within moments, Brenna's response came. "I'm bored at the library. Marlee says hi."

Kate's heart went out to the girl whom she'd learned so much about over the past two days. A minute later, Marlee had accepted her invitation.

Her message read, "RU OK?"

Kate stared at the letters for a second before she realized that they meant "Are you okay?"

She typed, "Yes, I'm just fine. Why?"

"Not many adults come on here" was the reply.

"I thought this would be a good way to get to know the youth group better now that my husband and I are taking over for Max." Then she had an idea. "Are you two coming on Sunday night?"

"We'll be there," Marlee typed, then "G2G."

Kate would definitely have to study her Internet slang if she was going to understand what these kids were saying.

She finished her invitations, then took a few minutes to study Brenna's and Marlee's pages. Both were basic, listing favorite TV shows and songs, with messages back and forth to their friends. Kate decided to study them in depth later when she had more time. There was bound to be some slipup, something that might confirm her suspicions about Marlee.

Then she made her way to the library's reference room, which was also on the second floor of the building. She decided to start with the Waters family, the other family Malcolm Dekker had mentioned.

Kate scanned the *Chronicle*'s indexes, searching for the name. There weren't any newspaper articles about them, other than the lone obituary, dated only two years earlier. Kate jotted down the names of the woman's three teenage daughters—Kim, Maureen, and Suzanne—along with their ages. According to her calculations, the youngest, Suzanne, would have been in ninth grade at the time of her mother's death, making her a junior this year.

Then she pulled out several of the small microfiche sheets dated ten years prior and began to scan for any mention of the Jones's tragic loss. It took several sheets before the obituary appeared on the screen.

It was dated October 4. There was a photograph of the young mother with the name "Maridee Jones" under it in bold letters. Kate read the short obituary that listed her parents; in-laws; husband David; and five-year-old Marlee, as her surviving family. She whispered the last line aloud to herself, glad there was no one else in the room. "Funeral services will be held October 6 at Faith Briar Church with interment at Mound Cemetery." Kate printed the page.

"I know where you're headed next," Livvy said with a grin from the doorway.

Kate chuckled when she realized that Livvy had heard her and knew exactly what she was thinking.

"Do you have some old phone books?" Kate asked as she wrote down the information from the Jones obituary.

"Phone books?"

Kate nodded.

Livvy led her to the reference section, but the phone books there were recent. "I need old ones, three years ago to last year's," Kate clarified.

"Sure, I'll go get them."

A moment later, Livvy returned with three Copper Mill phone books and handed them to Kate.

Kate paged through the *W*'s in the oldest volume, then scanned the other two before looking at Livvy.

"Riley Waters had a listing three years ago," she began, "but then nothing the year the mother died. Near as I can guess, they moved right after her passing."

"Or they got an unlisted number," Livvy suggested.

"I could understand a single mother making the number unlisted for safety reasons, but it doesn't seem as likely for a single father. Do you have last year's Copper Mill High yearbook?" She glanced at her notes from the microfiche.

Livvy gave her a "What are you up to now?" look, then led her to the shelves that held thirty years of Copper Mill's yearbooks.

Kate scanned the titles for the previous year's edition, paging through until she found the section for the sophomores, the grade Suzanne Waters, the youngest of Riley's children, would have been in that year. Kate studied the faces. Then for good measure, she looked through both the freshman and junior sections of the book. But there was no Suzanne Waters listed.

"They moved," she said simply, handing the book to Livvy.

"You've gotten good at this, haven't you?" Livvy laughed.

"A lot of it is pure instinct."

She tucked the obituaries into her handbag and said, "I think it's time to see what the cemetery has to offer."

MOUND CEMETERY on the outskirts of Copper Mill was like any cemetery in America—a quiet, peaceful place surrounded by popsicle-shaped trees as well as towering oaks.

The ground was a bit wet, since spring had just arrived, so Kate stepped carefully, glad she'd worn boots.

She walked the rows of headstones, beginning in the southeast corner and working her way methodically along the rows so she wouldn't miss any. There were headstones with crosses, but none with the telltale Celtic cross she was looking for. There were headstones with photographs of the deceased, and some with military honors. She passed row after row, then finally she saw the words she'd been looking for: "Maridee Jones—mother, wife, gone too soon." Below were the words "Never gone from our hearts," and beneath that was an ornate Celtic cross.

Chapter Seven

As she made her way back into town, Kate prayed for Marlee, imagining what it would be like to go through the stages of pregnancy alone as a young woman. With no one to talk to her about the changes in her body, and no one to tell her that everything would be okay, that her life wasn't over, that she still had a life to look forward to, that a baby *could* be a blessing.

She made her way to the Country Diner, where she was meeting Renee Lambert and Betty Anderson to discuss their part in the afterprom planning.

Kate had been thinking of Marlee ever since she'd seen the headstone. But her thoughts turned to Arlene Jacobs too. Perhaps after school was out, she'd head to the Mercantile to see if the mortician's niece was working.

The town gathering place, with its blue vinyl booths and blue gingham curtains, was filled with lunch patrons. The hum of their conversations filled the air. LuAnne Matthews flew from table to table.

Renee Lambert was already at a booth that looked out on the Town Green. She waved Kate over.

"Betty called and said to order without her," Renee said. "Sounded like she was running late."

Kisses poked his little head from the depths of her designer tote and gave a yelp of greeting as Kate sat.

"*Shh*," Renee murmured, petting him and setting his bottom deeper in the tote's depths. "I don't know what's up with him today. He keeps trying to get out of his tote." She leaned down to the pooch and said in a baby voice, "Does my Little Umpkins want to run around the restaurant today?"

The dog gave her a look that clearly said he thought she was nuts, then he settled down to sleep and was soon snoring.

"Cute outfit." Renee pointed to Kate's sailor-blue tunic with embroidered white daisies that wove around her torso.

"Thanks," Kate said. "It was a gift from my daughter Rebecca."

Kate scooted farther into the booth and glanced out at the spring day. The sky had become overcast and sleepy looking. A car motored slowly up the street.

"Makes you want to take a nap, doesn't it?" Renee said, following Kate's glance. "That's how I always feel when it's cloudy like this, like I should climb back in bed and sleep for a few hours, until the sun decides to make up its mind about getting up."

"I did that cost comparison," Renee said, reaching into a macramé bag she carried in addition to Kisses' domain, then pulling out a printed sheet of paper. She set the paper on the table and turned it for Kate to read. "Tony's is five cents a slice cheaper than making it ourselves," she went on. "Of course, it depends on the toppings and whether we would make the crust from scratch. But I based this on ready-made pizza dough at SuperMart in Pine Ridge and a regular pepperoni-and-extra-cheese pizza, which I think kids would prefer."

Kate nodded, impressed that Renee had already completed the task. "Then Tony's it is," Kate said with a smile.

She leaned back as Renee grinned, obviously satisfied with herself.

LuAnne came by their booth just then. "I'm sorry it's taken me so long to get over here," the plump, red-headed waitress said in her honeyed voice, looking at them over the top of her horn-rimmed glasses. "Do you want menus?"

Not waiting for an answer, she laid two of the tall menus on the table between them.

"I know what I want," Kate said with a glance at Renee.

LuAnne took the menus back and tucked them under her arm, then pulled out her pencil and order pad.

"I'll take the blackened-chicken salad," Kate said. "And can I get the dressing on the side?"

LuAnne nodded and turned to Renee.

"What's the soup today?" Renee asked.

"French onion."

"That sounds perfect."

Betty Anderson appeared at the booth then, a bit winded. Her cheeks were flushed, and she said, "Sorry I'm late. I had a perm job that went long."

Betty owned Betty's Beauty Parlor in town. She was a whirlwind of a woman, always ready with a smile and conversation.

She must've touched up her hair recently because her roots were blond like the rest of her hair, instead of dark like the tip of a matchstick.

"Did you run to get here?" Renee asked, leaning over to look at her more closely.

LuAnne moved aside so Betty could take a seat next to Kate.

Betty ignored Renee's question and looked at LuAnne. "I'll take the chef's salad. Does that come with cherry tomatoes?" she asked.

"It can." LuAnne winked at her, then left to place the order.

"So what are we talking about?" Betty asked.

"We were just talking about the food," Kate said.

"I wish I could help with more than just the fund-raising," Betty said. "But prom is one of my busiest times of the year at the salon."

"It's not *just* fund-raising," Kate said. "That's a huge part of the party." She sat back for a moment in thought. "To be honest, I think the biggest hurdle we face right now is getting the youth excited about it so they'll turn out and bring their friends. I mean, what's the point if the teens don't actually show up?"

Kate heard a whimpering sound from the other side of the table. Renee turned toward it and lifted her designer tote onto her lap. She patted Kisses' shivering head and slipped him a snack that she kept for him in her purse. The dog chewed eagerly, and little crumbs fell down his chest and into the tote. Then he disappeared inside the bag, and Renee set it back on the seat beside her.

Kate went on as if she hadn't been interrupted. "We need to recruit."

"I'll ask the high school if they can make an announcement over the intercom," Betty offered. "Maybe they'd let me put up some posters asking for volunteers too."

LuAnne returned with their orders, and they bowed their heads for a brief prayer before digging into their meals.

Kate took a bite of her blackened-chicken salad, following it with a taste of a soft bread stick that practically melted in her mouth.

There was a flurry of activity near the front door of the restaurant as a large bouquet of gerbera daisies came in, followed by the short delivery person who carried it.

"Is Betty Anderson here?" the man said.

Betty lifted her head, a look of shock on her face. "Did you say Betty Anderson?" she asked.

He looked at the card again and said, "Yep. That'd be the one."

Betty placed a hand on her chest and said, "How did you know to find me here?"

He set the beautiful bouquet of colorful flowers on the table between the ladies and said, "I stopped at the beauty shop, and Alicia said to bring it here. Said it'd be a bigger surprise." He shrugged as if unimpressed, then he turned to go.

Betty glanced at the others before she reached for the card that peeked out of the bouquet. Her brow furrowed as she read.

"Who is it from?" Renee asked, lifting her face and squinting her eyes.

"It doesn't say," Betty whispered as she glanced around the noisy diner. She handed the card to Kate.

"To a woman who inspires me," it began. "I've admired you for a long, long time." Kate turned the card over. The back was blank.

"It isn't signed," Kate said.

"I know." Betty looked perplexed. "My husband rarely does anything this romantic . . . ," she said.

"Maybe he's trying to spice things up?" Kate suggested.

Betty shook her head. "It doesn't seem like him. Don't get me wrong, he's very sweet. But flowers aren't his thing."

"Maybe a customer sent them?" LuAnne offered, coming to the table and wiping her hands on a towel.

"At the salon?" Betty guffawed. "I do mostly women's hair. Which of my clients would go to this much trouble? Morty Robertson?"

Kate pictured the retired man who volunteered regularly at the library. He had a lighthearted laugh and loved watching *Oprah*.

Renee laughed. "Morty is even less likely than Bob," she said, referring to Betty's husband.

"It doesn't have to be a man," Kate observed. "A woman could've written that too."

LuAnne's eyes flicked across the restaurant. "Maybe someone here?" she whispered.

"Maybe it's Mr. Hood." Renee nodded toward the good-looking widower, who was eating at the counter. He was a trim man who could often be seen playing tennis on the high-school tennis courts during the warmer months and

walking everywhere in town, even in the middle of winter. He
had sharp-looking silver hair and eyes so pale blue that they
were almost spooky. His head was bent as he read the *Copper
Mill Chronicle*.

"That's ridiculous," Betty said. "Besides, if you recall, I'm
married. Mr. Hood isn't that kind of admirer."

"Whoever it is will reveal himself," Kate added. "I mean,
why go to all the trouble of sending flowers if you can't take
the credit, right?"

Betty sighed and bent one of the stems to sniff their
earthy scent. "I guess you're right. And who knows, maybe my
husband did send them."

When the ladies turned their attention back to the table,
they watched in stunned silence as Kisses popped out of his
tote, hopped up on the table and buried his nose in Betty's
salad, munching away as if ravenous.

Betty shrieked. "Get your dog out of my food, Renee!"

Renee quickly grabbed the bug-eyed Chihuahua.

"Naughty dog," she scolded, but the tiny dog didn't look
right. His mouth was open, and he was gagging. "He's choking!" Renee's voice was panicked. "What do I do?"

Kate grabbed Kisses from across the table and gave him a
hard whack between the shoulder blades. A cherry tomato
shot out of the dog's mouth, fully intact. It landed on the
table behind them and rolled in front of a blue-haired customer, who gave it a disgusted look.

"Sorry," Kate said, reaching for the tomato with a napkin
so she wouldn't have to touch the slimy thing.

The dog was instantly revived. He gazed up happily at

Kate as if to say thank you, then with a bark, turned his mournful eyes toward Renee.

She pulled him from Kate's grasp and frantically petted his head.

"You hit him hard." She looked accusingly at Kate. "My poor baby. My poor baby."

"Your poor baby was eating *my* food," Betty said under her breath. "I hope you plan on buying me another salad."

LuAnne returned and asked what was wrong.

"Kisses almost died," Renee blurted out, tears streaming down her face, streaking her mascara.

"He ate my salad and choked on a cherry tomato," Betty clarified, her tone deadpan. "Can I get a new one?"

"Betty Anderson!" Renee said, placing a hand on her chest in shock. "I just hope your salad doesn't make him sick."

LuAnne scrunched up her face and glanced from Renee to Betty to Kate and finally said, "I'll see if there are any scraps we can dig up for you in the kitchen, Betty."

"Well!" Renee was indignant. She lifted the pooch to gaze into his mournful brown eyes. "Are you okay, Umpkins? He doesn't look right to me." She looked at Kate. "I need to take him to the vet."

"Renee, he's fine," Kate tried to reassure her.

"No." Renee was shaking her head. She reached for Kisses' tote, as well as her macramé bag and stood to go. "I'm taking him to Dr. Milt, and you're coming with me, Kate Hanlon. You did this to him."

Kate groaned inwardly, though she wanted to calm Renee. The dog was perfectly fine, but Kate knew that without a witness, Renee's story of woe would grow to monumental proportions. She gave Betty an apologetic look, then left to see what the good doctor had to say.

WHEN THEY ENTERED the squat brick building, Kisses began to whine. Renee pulled him close and made cooing noises in his ear.

"Mrs. Lambert? Can I help you?" the curly-headed receptionist said in a sweet-sounding voice. Then she nodded to Kate and said, "Mrs. Hanlon."

Her name tag read "Ashley Williams." Kate was surprised that she knew her by name, though they had met on a few occasions. She shared the receptionist's job with an older woman, whose name escaped Kate.

She had a young face, but she had a mature way of carrying herself, and the knitting needles in her hands suggested that she might be older. She was creating a long multicolored scarf with a cable stitch running down its length. Her face looked pale, and she had dark circles under her eyes. Kate studied the girl for a long moment.

"I need to get my baby in to see Dr. Milt," Renee said, holding up the dog in his tote for Ashley to see. "He just choked on a tomato!"

Ashley looked from Renee to Kate, the look of compassion on her face unmistakable. She clicked on her computer for a few moments, then said with a kind smile, "I think the doctor can squeeze you in if you'll take a seat."

Kate and Renee took their places in two of the hard plastic chairs in the waiting area. Renee was engrossed with

Kisses, who was sleeping in his designer tote and snoring. She stroked his head and cooed at him. Kate glanced back at the receptionist, who had disappeared down the long hall of examination rooms. She returned a few moments later with the short, bald-headed doctor following close behind.

"Renee?" he said, an echo of "What now?" in his voice.

"Dr. Milt." Renee rose and Kisses roused from his slumber. He looked from the doctor to Renee. "We were eating lunch at the Country Diner," Renee said, "and he choked on a tomato."

Kate stood.

Renee glanced at her as she continued. "Kate whacked him so hard on the back, I'm sure she gave him internal injuries."

"Did that dislodge the tomato?" the veterinarian asked.

"Well . . . yes," Renee admitted.

"Let's say we have a look," Dr. Milt said, placing a hand on Renee's shoulder and leading her to one of the examination rooms.

Kate followed, standing in the back of the room near the door, her arms crossed over each other in the slightly chilly air. The place smelled of antiseptic and the vague musky scent of animals.

Of course, there was nothing wrong with the tomato-thieving canine. Nonetheless, the veterinarian checked him out thoroughly, gazing deep into his throat and listening to his heart and lungs while Kisses shivered on the cold stainless-steel examining table.

Renee hovered like the nervous mother she was, her fingers fluttering then resting on her chest as she looked on.

Kate wondered if she was holding her breath. It was rare for Renee to be so quiet.

The doctor lifted the little dog's head and smiled. Renee finally let out a long breath, and she laughed in a way that spoke of relief.

Kate's gaze flicked to the door. She couldn't get her mind off of Ashley and how ill she looked. She glanced back at Renee, then deciding there wasn't much she could do to help anyway, said, "I'm going to head back to the waiting room."

Renee didn't acknowledge that she'd heard her. She was chattering on about how thankful she was, and it was really all so silly, but she just couldn't get the idea out of her head that something else might have happened to poor Kisses when he choked on that tomato and Kate hit him so hard . . .

The veterinarian met Kate's eye for an instant. His expression said, "Get out while you can," so she quickly made her way back down the long hall.

Ashley was still in her chair, but her head was in her hands.

"Are you okay?" Kate said when she reached the counter that overlooked the reception desk.

"Mrs. Hanlon." Ashley looked up, then confessed, "I haven't been feeling well all morning. It comes and goes, but . . ." She shrugged.

"Can I get you something? Do you feel nauseated?"

The girl nodded and lifted the empty plastic wastebasket that she had at the ready. "I hate this, but I can't afford to miss work. I've gotten so far behind as it is." She brushed her dark, curly hair from her face and held it behind her head like a ponytail. "You're so sweet to ask. I've always known that you

and Mr. Hanlon were nice people. He's been in here a few
times too, with Carl. He's always taken the time to talk and
ask questions about me and my folks. You're a lucky woman."

She must have been talking about Carl Wilson and his
cocker spaniel, Scout.

The comment about Paul struck Kate as odd. Not that
Paul wasn't a kind person, because, of course, he was very
kind. But Ashley seemed to know Paul and her so much better than they knew her. Ashley closed her eyes and rubbed
her cheeks as if a wave of nausea had struck again.

"I'm sorry," she whispered to Kate.

"You should go home and rest," Kate said, but Ashley
shook her head no.

"I'll be fine," she insisted. "This will pass. It always does."

Chapter Eight

After Renee had returned Kate to her car at the diner, it was two thirty. She made her way to the library to take advantage of the high-speed Internet connection and see if any new girls had joined her FriendsForever circle. A couple of the boys from youth group had accepted her invitation. Kate was amazed that the students had been on the site even in the middle of a school day.

She clicked on Brenna Phillips' profile page and looked around. The girl was raised by a single mother, so Kate knew she couldn't be the sender of the anonymous letter. But out of curiosity, she scrolled around the page anyway. There were several messages back and forth between Brenna and Marlee on their bulletin boards, so Kate clicked over to Marlee's page.

In the "Today I'm feeling . . ." space that gave members a chance to fill in the blank, Marlee had written "ready to snap." Kate paused over the words. Then she glanced at the "Relationship Status" section, and it said, "in a long-term relationship."

Kate needed to talk to the girl, she knew. So much evidence pointed her way, but she'd have to approach Marlee with a sensitive and loving spirit, and she'd have to choose the right moment.

Kate paused, then decided to post a message on her bulletin board.

Good afternoon, everyone,

This is a new thing for me, putting my thoughts out there on this public space. So you'll have to tell me how I'm doing. Once in a while, I'm going to post some thoughts—mostly on faith—that I've been processing. Here's one of those thoughts:

I've been thinking lately about the secrets we keep, the things we hold inside us and share with no one. We all have secrets, either big or small. Sometimes they're nothing more than a thought or a judgment toward another person. But sometimes they're big—something so life-changing that we'd be terrified if anyone knew what was really going on in our lives.

I want you to know that you can tell God anything. He won't be shocked or upset, or stop loving you. He already knows what's going on with each of us, even our innermost thoughts, and he accepts us and loves us, and forgives us.

I also want to tell you that while it might not seem like it, your parents want to be there for you. They want to know what's going on in your lives. Sometimes they might be disappointed, but I'm confident that they will

*always love you. They want to help you through the hard
spots. They really do.*

Love always,
Kate

Then she signed off. She hoped the message would spur
the girl to action, but she also knew that it was something
that everyone needed to be reminded of once in a while.

She had to go to the Mercantile to do some grocery shopping. She glanced at her watch. It was just after three o'clock.
The high-school-aged employees were probably making their
way to work about that time. With any luck, Arlene Jacobs
would be scheduled for the day.

Arlene wasn't at the checkout counter when Kate came
in, so she grabbed one of the plastic baskets near the front
door and moved along the aisles. She picked up a half gallon
of milk, a dozen eggs, and some cheese, then she moved
toward the bread aisle. She gazed down each aisle she
passed. No Arlene. She tossed a small loaf of wheat bread
into her basket. Finally, in the health-and-beauty aisle, she
found Arlene.

"Good afternoon, Arlene," Kate said.

The young bleached-blonde lifted her face and returned
the greeting.

"How are you?" Kate asked.

"Oh, I'm fine."

"I was talking to Malcolm Dekker the other day. I didn't
realize you were related," Kate began.

"Yup, we are. What did my weird uncle say now?" She

chuckled. "He means well, you know, but you can't take him too seriously. I think the strange personality goes with the job."

Kate laughed, recalling his comment about her looking for a new family. Then she sobered. "He has your picture on his desk."

Arlene nodded. "I gave that to him for Christmas a couple years ago. I guess it means a lot to him."

Kate watched her, trying to gauge whether she could be the letter writer.

"Anyway," Arlene said, obviously distracted. Then she picked up a box of feminine products and waved good-bye. "See ya later, Mrs. Hanlon!"

She had a little bounce in her step, and besides that, the young woman's purchase gave it away: the girl was *not* pregnant.

With Arlene checked off Kate's list, she decided to drop in at Emma's Ice Cream for a few minutes. With any luck, Marlee would be working that day too.

Kate entered, and several customers turned to greet her. She said "hello" in reply and made her way to the counter where Angie Petzel, Marlee Jones, and Anne Jackson were gathered in a circle, apparently deep in discussion. Kate could hear Emma humming in the back room.

Kate studied Marlee. The girl still looked tired and pale, and there were dark circles under her eyes.

Anne was saying, "Emma wants us to scrub down the freezer and do a thorough cleaning of the back today. That's why she scheduled us all at the same time." By the looks on their faces, Angie and Marlee weren't too enthused at the news.

"Hey, Mrs. Hanlon," Angie said, noticing Kate standing there. They paused their discussion and turned to her as a group. "Back for another cone?"

"I don't think so," Kate said. "Too many of those, and you'll have to roll me out of here."

"So what can we do for you?" Angie said. She had on a funky outfit in orange and brown paisley. *Funky* was the only word Kate could think of to describe it. The top was a knit with a hood, and the slacks were solid brown and flared at the bottom. The ensemble accentuated her tall, thin frame.

"Actually," Kate began. "I'm glad you're all together. I'm on the lookout for more afterprom helpers." She glanced at Marlee.

"Yeah, you talked about it at the meeting last night," Anne said.

"We've been talking about getting more students involved in the planning." She looked to Marlee and Angie. "What do a bunch of old fogies know about teenagers' likes and dislikes?" Kate paused, and the girls smiled at her. "We want to make sure we're putting energy into something you guys will be excited about."

The girls looked at each other as if trying to assess what the others would say before venturing out.

Angie was the first to speak up, "I'd love to help . . . if it's okay with my dad. He asked me to do some extra chores around the house, but I think I can handle it. I'll ask him when I get home."

"Fair enough," Kate said.

"What kind of things did you need us to do?" Marlee asked.

She was younger than the other two by a couple of years, and Kate could tell that she was eager to fit in, especially since she was technically too young to attend the prom. Marlee glanced between Angie and Anne, then back at Kate.

"Simple stuff, really," Kate said. "The car-wash fund-raiser next week." Anne nodded that she was already on board to help.

Kate went on, "The game booths will need to be painted; we need to put up posters around town, that kind of thing." She paused, not wanting to overwhelm the girls or seem too pushy.

"Sounds great," Angie said, her gaze meeting Kate's. "I had a lot of fun at the afterprom party in Pine Ridge a couple years ago."

"Yeah, it should be fun," Anne said. "Count me in."

Marlee said, "I'll see if I can get Brenna to help too." Then she shrugged. "I'm sure my dad won't care either way." The comment caused Kate to glance at the girl.

"Actually," Kate said, glancing between Angie and Marlee, "why don't you both send me a message on FriendsForever when you find out if you can come?"

She hoped Marlee would see the message about secrets that she'd posted earlier that afternoon.

KATE HAD A LOT ON HER MIND when she got home later that afternoon. It was four thirty. Paul would be home in half an hour, so she sprinkled a couple of chicken thighs and legs with thyme and salt and put them in the oven to roast. Then she pulled out a package of fresh brussels sprouts. She trimmed them, seasoned them with sea salt, and placed them in a small dish with some butter to bake. She set the dish aside to pop in the oven later, so it would finish along with the chicken. She had rolls and a dinner salad set to go. Since there was nothing else to do, she opened her laptop computer to connect to the Internet via the phone line in the kitchen.

The dial-up connection was impossibly slow. Kate tapped her fingers on the countertop while she waited. A hundred thoughts tumbled through her mind. She recalled the image of Ashley looking so pale and ill and her familiarity with Kate and Paul even though they barely knew her. Then she thought about Marlee's comment about her dad not caring whether she helped with the afterprom party, and her need to have Brenna at her side. They certainly seemed to be indicators that Marlee might be the girl who needed help.

Finally the FriendsForever log-in page appeared. Kate typed in her user name and password. Eight more teens had accepted her invitation to join her circle. Among them were James and Justin Jenner, Anne Jackson, and Angie Petzel.

There were also two messages in her in-box. The first was from Angie Petzel, saying that her father had said it was okay for her to help with some of the afterprom preparations as long as it didn't interfere with her other commitments.

Kate responded with, "I'm so glad you can join us."

Then, before reading the second message, she clicked on a friend request from the name that read "Mouse." Kate clicked Accept and followed the link to Mouse's page. There was no identifying information there. In the place of a photograph in the upper left-hand corner was an illustration of a mouse. It stood on its hind legs staring forward with its tiny arms outstretched.

Kate stared at the image for a long moment. *Mouse.* Kate clicked over to the girl's Friends tab. Only Kate's picture was there. She had no other friends, not a single link or message. It was a blank slate.

When Kate returned to her own page, she clicked on the In-box tab to read the message from "Mouse" that was waiting for her. She took a deep breath and began to read as she vaguely heard the sounds of Paul's truck in the driveway.

Dear Mrs. Hanlon,

I'm so glad that you created this FriendsForever page. I've been thinking about you and Pastor Hanlon ever since I sent you that first letter. I know you're someone who cares about people. I've seen all the things you do around town. And you're always so nice to me whenever I see you.

I went to the doctor today. I'd only taken one of those home tests before. But the doctor said it was true—I am going to have a baby. How can this be happening to me? The doc promised me that he wouldn't tell anyone. Said something about doctor-patient privilege. I hope that's true. I hope he doesn't go telling my dad. I am more afraid than ever of what my dad will do when he finds out. But he'll find out soon enough, won't he? And my boyfriend—I can't even think about what he'll say. I'm too young for this. I'm not ready to be a mother! The truth is, I still need a mother myself.

This is all my fault. If I'd been a better person, this wouldn't have happened.

Mouse

Kate stared at the last comment. Her heart broke for this girl. To go to a doctor all alone, knowing the news he would tell her, must have been torture. Kate placed a hand lightly on the screen and closed her eyes.

"Oh, Father," the prayer welled up of its own accord. "This young woman needs encouragement, and courage, but most of all, she needs a friend. I want to be that to her. But I am comforted to know that you are the best of friends. You stick closer than a brother. Please do that for her. Amen."

She opened her eyes to see Paul standing across the kitchen counter, staring at her, a question in his eyes.

"I got an e-mail from the girl, Mouse," she said simply, turning the laptop so Paul could read it. Kate watched his blue eyes track across the page.

When he lifted his gaze, she saw the same concern in his eyes that she felt for this young girl.

He shook his head. "What are you going to tell her?"

"That she still has reason to hope."

Chapter Nine

Kate kissed Paul on the forehead and headed to choir practice at Renee Lambert's house. The choir met there every Wednesday evening for rehearsal. Kate didn't consider herself much of a singer, but her voice wasn't awful either. Since Faith Briar was a small congregation and had less of a talent pool to draw from, she'd joined the choir, singing alto.

Kate pulled up in front of Renee's house and walked up to the door. She knocked briefly to announce her arrival, then let herself in. The dozen or so members chatted here and there in clusters of conversation.

Renee's home was beautifully decorated in shades of mauve, ivory, and pale green, with a classic sensibility.

When everyone had gathered on folding chairs that were set up in the large living room, Sam started the rehearsal. He played organ and motioned sometimes with a dip of his head, sometimes with a raised hand to let the choir know when to come in. The movement of his slightly swaying body helped them to keep the beat.

Renee's elderly mother, Caroline Beauregard Johnston, sat in the very back of the room with her arms crossed in front of her and a perpetual scowl on her wizened face. Kisses meandered past, and the woman swatted at him, causing the dog to scurry into the kitchen.

When Sam had gone through several songs, Renee moved to the front. "I'm directing this song since Sam will be out of town next Sunday," Renee reminded as she held up a copy of the sheet music for them to get out of their folders.

Sam Gorman rarely called on Renee to fill in for him as choir director, though she was fairly good when she set her mind to it and wasn't acting as though she was the director of the Nashville Symphony.

"Now, everyone. Eyes up here."

Kate caught Sam's gaze. A grin spread across his face, and he nodded to Renee, who tapped the white baton on the top of her music stand.

The next Sunday's piece, which they'd been rehearsing off and on for the past two months, was an ambitious yet beautiful song titled "He Took the Cup."

Renee's arm moved with each beat while Sam Gorman kept up on Renee's little organ. Betty Anderson stood on one side of Kate, singing in her high-pitched slightly nasal voice, with Livvy Jenner on the other side, singing alto in her pretty Karen Carpenter-like voice.

They ran through several more songs, and Renee handed out a new piece, which they stumbled through awkwardly just once before returning to the next Sunday's music one last time.

When the song ended, Sam gave a satisfied smile. "That wasn't half bad," he said. Then he cleared his throat. "At least I think the congregation won't throw rotten tomatoes at you."

"That's easy for you to say," Betty Anderson quipped. "You won't be there." A chuckle erupted from the group.

Everyone passed their sheet music to the end of each row, and LuAnne Matthews set the stack on the coffee table.

Renee motioned to her mother, who was now standing at the back of the room. "Mother has some treats for us in the dining room if you can stay."

Kate closed her folder and glanced at her watch. It was still fairly early, so she decided that a little visiting would do her good.

The choir gathered around the dining-room table, where Renee's mother was setting tea and scones out for a snack.

More than half of the choir members excused themselves, so there was a smaller group than usual that night.

Kisses yipped at people's feet, and Caroline hissed at him to scat, then she thrust her jeweled cane at him, but the dog was undaunted. He bared his teeth at the elderly woman, and then when Renee's back was turned, Kate saw Caroline give him a little kick in the hindquarters. Not too hard, but just enough to cause Kisses to run to his dog bed in the corner of the living room.

Kate reached for a pretty china plate with tiny roses around the edge from the stack on the white tablecloth, then helped herself to a scone with a dab of whipped cream and settled down next to Livvy in the living room with a cup of Renee's signature Earl Grey tea.

"Did you find out who sent the flowers?" LuAnne asked Betty.

The bleached-blonde beautician shook her head. "And

Bob was none too happy when I walked in the door with that big bouquet in hand."

"Why?" Kate said, taking a sip of her tea.

"He thinks I have a secret admirer." She shook her head. "I haven't seen him this upset since we were first dating, and another boy asked me to the prom!"

Renee took the seat on the other side of Betty and LuAnne on the couch.

"Did you tell Livvy about what happened today with Kisses?" Renee said to Kate, paying no heed to the previous discussion.

Livvy looked blankly at Kate, who shook her head, but Renee didn't need permission to continue. She launched into the tale immediately, telling about the dog's fateful tomato dislodgement.

"Kate hit Kisses so hard, I thought she'd knocked him unconscious."

"She did save your dog's life, Renee," LuAnne reminded her.

"Excuse me," Betty said, leaning to look Livvy in the eye. "Renee left out the part about Kisses climbing on top of the table in the middle of the diner and eating my salad."

"Well," Renee said, acting offended at their barbs, though Kate knew full well she was enjoying the attention. "My poor Kisses. I was certain something terrible had happened. Maybe he'd had a lack of oxygen to the brain from having that tomato in his windpipe or Kate had broken something in his little body. Who knows what could've happened."

Renee's mother took a seat at the other end of the living room. Kate heard her mutter, "We all know who had a lack of oxygen to the brain."

But Renee either didn't hear the comment or simply ignored it as she continued her story.

"Kate and I rushed Kisses to Dr. Milt's. He was right there to usher us back to the examination room." It wasn't exactly how Kate recalled it. "Well, don't you know it, Kisses was fine as rain. Not a thing wrong with him."

At hearing his name, the miniature dog lifted his head, tilting it from one side to the other.

"Isn't he just darling?" Renee gushed.

Caroline harrumphed, then took a sip of her Earl Grey.

"It was a nice excuse for me to say hi to Ashley Williams," Kate said, wondering if anyone knew the girl better than she did. "She's a really sweet girl."

"Did you see how much weight that girl has gained?" Renee said. "And she looked so peaked. I remember her when she was in high school. She was a twig of a thing, and now . . ."

"She's hardly fat, Renee," Kate scolded.

"No, but I bet she's put on a good twenty pounds in the past few months."

The image of the girl's pale face flashed before Kate, then of Ashley holding that wastebasket because she felt sick to her stomach.

"I take Kisses in there all the time," Renee continued. "I saw her when I took him in for his checkup in January, and she was fairly thin then." Renee turned to Betty and went on, "I hear she was seeing Carl Wilson. I was in there once when he brought that dog of his in, and you should've seen how she lit up when she saw him."

"When she saw the dog or Carl?" LuAnne asked. Kate was already distracted by Renee's comment.

"Speaking of young people, my stylist has been acting so bizarre lately," Betty said.

Kate turned to look at Betty.

"You know Ronda . . ." Betty went on. "She's usually a little late to work but lately she's been coming in later and later. Sometimes she leaves for no reason at all. It's downright embarrassing. She's left customers sitting in the chair unattended while she disappears to who knows where. She leaves the shop altogether! I've had to take over her work for her." She shook her head. "I don't know what I should do. She's a good beautician, but if this keeps up, I might have to let her go."

Just when Kate thought she was narrowing down the pool, another suspect surfaced. It was enough to drive her batty.

"I've known her since she was a little girl," Betty went on. "It'll just devastate her, but I can't run a business this way."

"She used to come in and watch me cut when she was younger. Didn't have an appointment herself or anything. She'd just sit in the front chair with her eyes glued while I cut and colored and permed. I knew she was hooked."

She smiled, then her expression became pained. "And she's been looking poorly. Her eyes are always red, like she's crying all the time, and if you look at her cross-eyed, she'll likely snap at you."

The e-mail had said that Mouse appreciated how friendly Kate was. And Kate knew Ronda from her visits to Betty's

Beauty Shop. The girl had always been amiable and had made conversation.

But how much did she really know about Ronda other than the fact that she was a stylist and was gifted at back-combing? She didn't even know if Ronda attended church.

"Have you asked her about it?" Kate inquired. She leaned over the coffee table and took another bite of her scone.

Betty nodded. "Oh, sure I've asked her. She acts dumb or changes the subject like she doesn't want to talk about it. Or she'll leave the room with some excuse about restocking the back shelves."

Kate looked at Livvy, who was talking to Sam in a side conversation.

"I know an excuse when I hear one," Betty said. "And this girl is up to something. I'm worried about her. More than whether she's doing a good job at the salon, I'm worried about *her*."

Chapter Ten

B y the time Kate finally got into her car to head for home, it was closing in on eight forty-five. All the businesses in town were closed, their windows darkened except for the occasional security light. A few cars were still parked in front of St. Lucy's Episcopal and Copper Mill Presbyterian on Smoky Mountain Road.

Kate kept thinking about the various young women she'd encountered that day. Was she spinning her wheels by suspecting every girl she saw? Or was the girl in need indeed among them?

Kate tightened her grip on the steering wheel as her frustration mounted. It seemed that almost every young woman in town had become a suspect. Did that say something about an innate lack of trust on her part? Or did she simply understand that human nature was weak, and everyone was capable of making missteps?

She pulled into her driveway and then picked up her cell phone and called Livvy.

"Did you catch the same things I did tonight?" she asked.

"What do you mean?"

"Well, first Renee says that Ashley Williams has gained a lot of weight, and then Betty goes on about Ronda, laying out many of the signs of pregnancy."

Livvy gasped. "Oh, wow, Kate, you're right. Those may not be coincidences."

"Exactly, but we have to narrow it down."

"Let's talk it out," Livvy said in her pragmatic way.

Kate walked up the walkway toward the door as she spoke, "Well, there's Marlee Jones. She was the first one Max mentioned. Raised by a single father, acting moody and sad, and secretive lately. She called in sick to work and mentioned her father's ambivalence toward her involvement in the after-prom party, and, of course, there was the Celtic cross on her mother's grave."

Kate pictured Marlee's freckled face and exuberant laugh. She would cover her mouth as if she didn't want anyone to see the silver braces on her teeth, but it didn't keep her from enjoying her friends. That was what had been so different about her the previous Sunday. Instead of that outgoing, vivacious teen, she'd been quiet and tearful. Kate had seen how she'd wiped the wetness away.

"Her FriendsForever page says she has a boyfriend. I wonder who it is," Kate said.

"I have no idea."

"She's seen us around church at least a few times. Someone like her would be more likely to open up to us than some of the other girls."

"That's true," Livvy conceded.

"So far, Marlee's the one who fits most of the clues," she

went on, not wanting to lose her train of thought. "Maybe I can ask Brenna a few questions tomorrow. I know they're good friends. And there's Ashley at the vet clinic," Kate added.

"There's a lot about her that fits the description too," Livvy agreed. "The weight gain, the nausea."

"And she acted like she knew me," Kate said. "Like she wanted to confide in me. It felt out of place."

"Is she dating Carl Wilson?"

"I'll ask Paul. He and Carl are friends, so he would know."

"Is there anyone else?" Livvy asked.

Kate pushed open the door and stepped gratefully into the house.

"Angie, but she doesn't seem to fit the girl in the letter. Angie's very self-assured, confident. Hardly the timid girl who wrote . . . And, of course, there's Ronda," Kate said. "Maybe I should have her do my hair."

"I was just starting to think the same thing," Livvy said.

"Whoever this girl is, she's having to do a lot of acting these days. She's bound to slip up somewhere."

Kate hung up her coat and wandered into the kitchen.

"Thanks for helping me think this through," Kate said.

"I'll get back to you if anything comes to me," Livvy said.

Kate said good-bye and hung up. She stood there a moment in silence. Her quest was putting her in touch with several young women who could benefit from the friendship of an older woman. Whether or not any of these women was the girl in question, the budding friendships were a good thing not only for them but for Kate too. To gain their fresh perspectives on the world would only help her to understand and empathize more—something she was always eager to do both as a youth leader and as a mother. It was the same way God reached down to humankind—by getting involved in their everyday lives.

The house was quiet. Paul had gone to a meeting of the area pastors that he attended regularly. Usually they met at the Country Diner if the meeting took place during the day, but that night they had decided to meet at one of the other churches, since they had invited a few pastors and elders from churches in Pine Ridge.

Kate caught a glimpse of her reflection in the kitchen window. Her strawberry blonde hair was getting a bit long, and her gray roots were peeking out more than she liked.

Yes, she decided, she would definitely see about having Ronda give her a touch-up.

ONCE SHE'D WARMED UP SOME SOUP and eaten, Kate decided to give Ashley Williams a call. What could it hurt to ask how she was feeling after the way she'd looked that afternoon? If she was Mouse, maybe a call would encourage her to speak up. If not, Kate could at least show that she cared about the receptionist by checking in on her and asking if she needed anything.

She picked up the thin community phonebook and looked up Ashley's number. There was nothing listed under Ashley Williams, but there was an Edward Williams. Kate wondered if it was the girl's father.

She glanced at the clock. It was nine. Deciding it wouldn't be too late, she dialed the number. It rang several times before an elderly sounding female voice came over the line.

"Williams' residence," the woman said.

"Hello, this is Kate Hanlon. Is this where I can find Ashley Williams?"

"Sure it is, dearie." Then her voice was muffled as Kate heard her call, "Ashley Jane. It's for you."

Finally Kate heard the girl's sweet voice on the line. "Hello?"

"Ashley," Kate began. "It's Kate Hanlon. I was just thinking about you, so I thought I'd give you a call to see if you're feeling better." Kate hoped she didn't come off as too intrusive.

"Oh, thank you," Ashley said. "I'm feeling much better. It's so sweet of you to call. I've always had a weak stomach. But I feel much better now."

"Oh good," Kate said. "Also, have you heard about the afterprom party that Faith Briar is hosting this year?"

"Everyone's heard about it; should be a great time. It's wonderful that the church is doing that for the high schoolers."

"I've been trying to drum up some younger volunteers to help out with decorating and the car wash, that kind of thing."

"You know, it's funny you should mention that," Ashley said. "I've been thinking of ways to get more involved in the community. Carl said that he was making the booths."

"Carl?" Kate said, a bit surprised at how easily his name fell from her lips.

"Yeah. You know, my folks have been nagging me to get out more. They say I spend too much time taking care of them."

"You take care of your parents?"

"They're getting on in years," Ashley explained. "I came along when they were pretty old already, and since I'm an only child, everything falls on me. Dad has Parkinson's disease, and it's getting harder and harder for Mom to take care of him. We want to keep him out of a nursing home as long as we can."

"Bless your heart," Kate said.

"Thankfully the disease is progressing at a fairly slow rate. It can turn bad quickly for some folks, you know."

Kate felt an immediate affinity for the girl. To care so willingly for her parents and not think of herself.

"So," Ashley was saying, "When is the next meeting? I'd be happy to come."

"It's next Tuesday at five o'clock at the church. Faith Briar up on Mountain Laurel Road."

"I know where it is. I'll be there, and thanks, Mrs. Hanlon, for everything."

Chapter Eleven

The next morning as Kate read her Bible a verse from Proverbs gave her pause. It read, *"I guide you in the way of wisdom and lead you along straight paths."*

Kate chuckled at God's sense of humor. The path to finding Mouse had been all *but* straight. Yet she knew that God had a purpose and would provide the wisdom she lacked. She closed her eyes, her heart heavy for the girl, and prayed. In the midst of her prayer, a thought came to her, an echo of her words from the night before.

As soon as she was sure Livvy was up and getting ready for work, Kate dialed her friend at home.

"Do you have church directories at the library?" she asked without preamble.

"I . . . uh . . . ," Livvy stammered. "Yes, we have some."

"How about Faith Community in Pine Ridge?"

"Yes, I think so."

"Okay, perfect. I'll be by first thing to pick it up."

Kate arrived at the library parking lot at the same time Livvy did. Livvy's purse was slung over her shoulder and her light jacket attested to the morning coolness that still clung to the valley.

Livvy gave her a puzzled look. "What is this about?" she asked as they walked up to the side entrance together.

"Just a hunch." Kate followed her in and waited while Livvy rummaged through a metal file cabinet in the back. Finally she emerged with a thin booklet in her hands. The front bore the image of a modern-looking church building— a simple line drawing.

Kate paged through the directory, looking for a familiar name.

There was a single Jones—Sarah—listed as residing in the Pine Ridge nursing home. Kate pulled a small notebook and pen from her handbag and wrote down the nursing home's central phone number.

"Who is Sarah Jones?" Livvy asked, looking over her shoulder.

"I'm not sure yet. I'm wondering if she's related to Marlee."

Kate pulled her cell phone from her handbag and dialed the number.

The phone rang only once before a pleasant-sounding voice came on the line. "Pine Ridge Nursing Home."

"Hello, this is Kate Hanlon. I'm Pastor Hanlon's wife. I'm calling to inquire about Sarah Jones."

"Sarah's doing much better now," the woman said.

"She has family in Copper Mill, right?" Kate asked, know-ing the question was leading.

"Oh yes. Her son David, and her granddaughter. Marlee is her name. Sweet girl."

Kate lifted her face to Livvy and nodded.

"Is Sarah up for visitors?"

"Sarah loves visitors."

PINE RIDGE WAS A BUSTLING TOWN. It boasted a SuperMart and a college, with many of the amenities that came with having a school. Kate made her way through the streets, stopping at a red light before pulling into the Pine Ridge Nursing Home community's parking lot.

Kate reached for the bouquet of flowers she'd picked up as a gift for the elderly woman, then made her way to the front desk. A petite redhead lifted her face to Kate and smiled.

"How can I help you?" she said in the same perky voice Kate had heard on the phone.

"I'm the one who called earlier about Sarah Jones."

"Oh yes." The woman rose to her feet and motioned for Kate to follow her. "She should be in her room," she said over her shoulder.

They passed a large, empty dining room, where women in hairnets were clearing dishes from the tables, and entered a tiled hallway, where a lost-looking man wandered between the rooms, muttering something under his breath. Kate said hello to him and offered a kind smile.

The redheaded receptionist paused in front of a room and knocked as she slowly opened the door.

The room was dark, save for the blue light of a television.

"Sarah," the woman said, "you have a visitor."

Kate stepped inside, her eyes adjusting to the subdued lighting. A thin form lay beneath white blankets, barely making a bulge in the bedding.

"Sarah," the woman repeated. "You have a visitor."

The silver-haired woman turned her face toward them and looked at Kate. "Do I know you?"

"We've never met, no. I'm a friend of your granddaughter Marlee's." Kate came alongside the hospital bed and set the bouquet of flowers on the bedside table.

"They're beautiful," Sarah said. She patted Kate's hand. "Any friend of Marlee's . . ."

"I'll head out," the receptionist said. "Do you want me to send someone in to get you out of bed, Sarah?"

"No," Sarah said, her gaze still on Kate, "I need my rest. We'll have a little visit right here. Is that okay?"

"Of course, it's okay," Kate said.

Before she left, the redhead pulled a folding chair from Sarah's closet and set it up for Kate alongside the bed. Kate thanked her and then turned to the elderly woman.

"So, how do you know my Marlee?" Sarah said.

"She comes to the youth group that my husband and I lead in Copper Mill."

"Has my Marlee been okay lately?"

Kate was surprised at the question.

"Why do you ask?"

"She hasn't been acting herself." Sarah shook her head. "Poor thing. She gets so upset sometimes—and who can understand the mind of a teenager? I worry about her, without me there when she gets home from school . . ."

"So you live with Marlee and her dad?"

"Oh yes. Well, I did. Ever since her mother died. I don't think David would've been able to manage without me there. Now that I'm in this place . . ."

"Do they have a home church that can help them?"

Sarah shook her head, sadly. "David stopped going to church when his Maridee died. They had come to Faith Community with me before . . . but no more." She inhaled a heavy breath. "That's why it's so good she's at least coming to your youth group."

"It sounds like you're worried about her."

The woman nodded. "Yes, I worry about Marlee a lot."

TALKING TO MARLEE'S GRANDMOTHER had only been a hunch, Kate reminded herself as she made her way to the clinic on the other side of town. But she needed to dig deeper. Mouse had said that she'd finally gone to the doctor for confirmation of her pregnancy. Kate knew that the likelihood of anyone at the clinic sharing information with her was nonexistent, but she had to at least make the effort. Maybe there would be some sign there to point in the right direction. What that would be, Kate wasn't quite sure yet.

When she reached the clinic, a man greeted her at the check-in desk. "Can I help you?" he said.

"Yes," Kate began, speaking low so no one else in the waiting room would hear her request. "Yesterday, I think it was, a girl came in for a pregnancy test . . ." She prayed the man would pick up the conversation. Instead, he gave her a blank stare.

"I'm wondering if you can help me locate her," Kate went on.

"I'm sorry, ma'am, but because of privacy laws, I'm not at
liberty to give out any information about our patients. Are you
her mother?"

"No. Would it make a difference if I was?"

"I'm afraid not."

"This girl sent me a couple of anonymous messages—
pleas for help. I was just hoping you could point me in the
right direction. I'm not trying to interfere. I want to help her."

The man sighed, and there was a long silence as he
glanced around the room.

"I won't tell her family or anyone she doesn't want to
know," Kate promised. "I'm just concerned about her."

"If she wanted you to know who she was, she would've
told you," the man said.

It wasn't as if that same thought hadn't occurred to Kate
before.

"I think she's too afraid to tell me," Kate said, though she
knew that he was speaking the truth. "But she's trying. That's
what her messages are about. She's searching for someone
who will care enough to help her."

"I appreciate your concern," the man said. "It's simply out
of my hands."

Kate breathed deeply, feeling a sense of sorrow overcome
her. So this was how it worked? Her heart ached for what this
girl was going through alone.

"Well, thank you for your time," Kate started.

"I'll only say," the man drew closer to her and lowered his
voice.

Kate leaned forward, not wanting to miss a word he was
about to say.

"She was from Copper Mill and too young to be having a baby."

"Oh. Okay," Kate said, feeling deflated that he hadn't offered her anything she didn't already know. She thanked him, then turned to leave. So much for narrowing down her options.

KATE MADE IT BACK to Copper Mill around noon, feeling tired and needing to rethink her strategy. She checked her e-mail on Paul's desktop computer, and then her FriendsForever messages to see if Mouse had answered her posting.

There were no new messages of any importance, though most of the teens she'd invited to be her friends had signed on. It was silly, but seeing their names alongside hers with the tab My Friends made her feel good. She supposed that was why people were so into this kind of thing—the feeling that others wanted to be their friend, that they mattered.

She decided to write a message on her bulletin board, which was an open posting spot, as opposed to her in-box, which was private.

Kate wrote, *Thanks to everyone who's signed on to be my friend. It feels good. I want to invite you to youth group this Sunday evening and invite your friends. It would be great to see you; I promise, you'll have fun! Kate.*

When she signed off, she glanced down at her day planner, which lay open on Paul's desk. Sunlight streamed in through the window, warming her. She turned to the next week, noting Kim and Chad Lewis' next counseling session for the following Monday.

She wondered how the couple was doing. Had they taken

to heart Paul's words? Had they followed through and made a set of ground rules to abide by? Kate hoped so, for their sakes. No matter how difficult it might be, the reward in the end was worth it.

Kate closed her eyes and prayed for the couple.

KATE DECIDED TO HEAD to the vet clinic again just after lunch. While her thoughts stayed with Marlee, she also kept imagining Ashley bent over that wastebasket.

The dark-haired girl raised her head when Kate came in. "Mrs. Hanlon, what brings you here?" Her smile was genuine, like everything else about the girl, and her eyes sparkled.

"I've been thinking about you ever since yesterday. I thought I'd stop in and say hello."

"I'm fine, really. Thanks for calling last night, by the way. That was sweet of you."

"It was my pleasure." Kate paused, hoping her next question wouldn't seem strange. "So, Ashley, out of curiosity, what are your plans for the future? Have you been to college?"

The young woman shrugged. "No, not yet. I've thought about it. I still might go, actually, but it's hard to say. I've always thought about becoming a dental hygienist; they can find work anywhere. Kind of like a teacher. I enjoy helping people." She shrugged her shoulders. "But I'm happy where I am for now."

In the short time that they'd been talking, Ashley's complexion had gone from rosy and healthy looking to ashen and pale. Ashley touched a hand to her perspiring forehead.

"I'm sorry," she said.

"Are you okay?"

Ashley reached into a drawer and pulled out a granola bar that she had stashed there. "Lately ..." She let the sentence drop, and she placed a hand on her chest as she closed her eyes.

"You feel nauseous again?"

"A little. Nothing a little food in my stomach won't cure. This time of day is always the worst."

The phone rang, and Ashley reached for it, saying in a weak voice, "Veterinarian's office. Can I help you?" Then she mouthed to Kate, "I'll be okay."

Kate hated leaving her in that condition, but the girl waved good-bye and turned her attention to her work. Kate stood there for a few moments, trying to decide what to do. As she stared, she noticed the notepad on Ashley's right. It was covered in drawings, some of them quite good.

A client came in with a gray and white domestic shorthair cat, bringing it to the high counter. He glanced at Kate and then at Ashley, who lifted a finger to tell him it would only be a minute.

Kate waved good-bye and stepped out into the sunshine.

She was worried about the girl, so she lifted her face and closed her eyes. *Lord,* she prayed silently, *something isn't right with Ashley. Help her. You saw the way she looked. If she is Mouse, please help me to help her. If it's Marlee or Ronda at the beauty salon, Lord, please show me.*

Chapter Twelve

Kate stopped by the beauty salon to make an appointment with Ronda, but the next available slot wasn't until the following Tuesday. With an afterprom meeting scheduled for that evening, Kate knew it would be tight, but she went ahead and made the appointment anyway.

Then she went home where she called Brenna Phillips. The girl sounded winded, as if she'd had to run to get to the phone.

"Hi, Brenna, this is Kate Hanlon."

"Hi, Mrs. Hanlon! What's up? I just got home from school."

"Oh perfect. Do you have time to chat?"

"Sure." There was a long silence.

"I mean." Kate cleared her throat. "Could I meet with you? Maybe by the swings at Copper Mill Park. It's such a nice day."

"Okay," she drew the word out, obviously leery of an adult wanting to get together to talk, but she agreed to meet Kate at three thirty nonetheless.

BRENNA WAS SWINGING on one of the swings in the park when Kate arrived. It was a warm day for early April. Still, Brenna was wearing a red hooded sweater with the Copper Mill High School logo on the front. A white T-shirt was peeking from the neckline, and her hip-looking jeans were tucked into brown knee-high boots.

"I hope you don't mind coming to meet me," Kate said, leading her to one of the benches that faced the play area.

"I wasn't doing anything right now anyway," Brenna said.

Kate wasn't sure where to begin, so she decided to go with the innocuous. "I heard that you and Marlee were chosen to be prom servers," she said.

Prom servers were high-school students who were too young to attend prom but were selected by the juniors and seniors to serve punch and food and thus partake of the festivities.

Brenna's face lit up. "I'm so excited. Marlee and I have been studying every dress catalog we can get our hands on!" She laughed. "Did you go to prom, Mrs. Hanlon?"

"Oh yes," Kate said. "I'm the one who asked my date to go, which was unheard of in my day."

Brenna's eyes grew large with that bit of information.

"My date had a golf meet the afternoon before prom," Kate went on, "and ended up missing the grand march! I wasn't happy about coming out unescorted, and I didn't let him forget it. Poor guy." Kate laughed at the memory.

Brenna covered her mouth as she giggled. Then she asked, "It's okay that Marlee and I are coming to the afterprom party even though we're technically too young to go to the prom?"

"Of course, it's okay. It'd be wrong to ask you to help and then not let you attend," Kate said.

Brenna smiled. "We wouldn't want to end the evening too early, you know?" She looked at Kate.

The conversation ebbed, and Kate knew she needed to bring their talk around to the reason she'd come in the first place.

"There is a reason I asked you to meet me," Kate confessed.

Brenna sat up straight.

"I wanted to ask you some questions about Marlee. How well do you know her?"

"She's a good friend."

"I heard that her mother died."

"When she was little." Brenna nodded. "It was so hard for her. That's how we became such good friends. I could relate to having only one parent."

Kate looked Brenna in the eyes. "Has she been acting . . . odd lately?"

"Yeah, actually. Something's going on that she isn't telling me about. I thought maybe she and her boyfriend broke up."

"Who's her boyfriend?" Kate asked.

"I've never met him. He's an older boy from Pine Ridge. Is Marlee in trouble?"

"I don't know," Kate said.

Brenna chewed her lower lip. "She's having a hard time coping with something. Usually she'd tell me." She shrugged, but her eyes reflected her deep concern.

"What's her relationship with her father like?" Kate asked.

Brenna's brows knitted together. "Why do you want to know that?"

"I'm just curious."

"She and her dad are really close. It's the most important relationship in Marlee's life, for sure. That and her relationship with her grandma."

KATE FINISHED WASHING the supper dishes that night. Paul had helped with the bulk of the work, but she'd wanted to clean under the sink after putting everything away. He'd meandered into the living room to watch a documentary on Alaskan dogsled races.

Kate plopped onto the couch next to him and watched for a few minutes. When the show went to commercial, she said, "Honey, do you have a sec for a question?"

Paul turned to look at her. "Of course, Katie. What's up?"

"By any chance, do you know if Carl Wilson is dating anyone?"

"Why? Did you have someone in mind to set him up?"

Kate laughed. "No. Renee mentioned that she thought he was going out with Ashley Williams from the vet clinic."

"You think Carl and Ashley could be the couple from the letter?" He raised an eyebrow.

Kate shrugged. "I don't know. The letter did say the boyfriend is older."

"I could find a way to ask, I guess."

"Thanks," Kate said.

The show came back on the air, and their conversation faded in favor of it. But Kate couldn't concentrate on it. She retrieved the girl's letter from the sorter on the kitchen counter and reread it.

She studied the loopy script with hearts for dots above the *i*'s and the drawing of the Celtic cross in the lower corner. One statement stood out: "My dad will . . . kick me out of the house."

Was that the statement of a girl who was close to her father?

She glanced up at Paul, who flicked off the TV and stood.

"I'm going to do a bit of work in the study," he said.

"Okay. I think I'll check my e-mail messages. Are you going to need the phone line?"

Paul said no, then disappeared into his study.

Pulling out her laptop, she connected to the kitchen's phone line and dialed in to open Mouse's last e-mail. She read it through, feeling the tug of empathy that had come with the first reading. Then she read the previous night's reply before writing another message to the girl.

Dear Mouse,

I can't tell you how glad I am that you e-mailed me. I'm here to be your friend and to tell you not to give up. Yes, your life will be changed by a baby, but it doesn't have to be a devastating event. Children, no matter how they come into this world, are precious. And God offers forgiveness to everyone who asks. He loves you. I hope you know this to be true deep inside, because even when you feel unloved by your father or your boyfriend or even yourself, you need to know that your heavenly Father thinks you're something special. Don't forget that, okay?

Your friend,
Kate

Kate read back through the post a couple of times, wanting to make sure it held the right balance of encouragement and truth, then when she was satisfied, she hit Send.

FRIDAY PASSED into Saturday. There was no reply from Mouse. Kate kept busy around the house, though there was something indefinable that nagged at her. She couldn't put her finger on it, yet it was there.

Paul had driven his pickup to Pine Ridge to shop for more fishing supplies, so Kate gathered her laptop and set it up in Paul's study. She logged onto FriendsForever and scanned the opening page that gave blurbs about Kate's friends, indicated whether they'd updated their sites or added photos, commented on this or that.

She moved to her in-box.

Her heart jumped when she saw a message from Mouse with the subject line, "I think I'm losing the baby." The time stamp said it had been sent forty minutes earlier.

Kate hurried to click on the message.

There was no introductory line, simply,

I'm spotting and cramping. It's not a lot, but it is there. I don't know what to do. As much as I hate being in this position, the thought of losing this baby scares me even more. What should I do? I need to do something, don't I?

Okay, I just called the hospital, and they told me I have to be seen by a doctor. Pray for me, okay? Pray real hard.

Mouse

Kate's heart was in her throat. She swallowed, staring at the words. She had to go to Mouse. She glanced back at the time stamp. Forty minutes. Perhaps she could still make it.

Kate flew to her car and tossed her handbag onto the passenger seat before turning on the ignition and peeling out of the driveway. She took a deep breath and reminded herself to slow down. Getting a speeding ticket would only eat more time out of her trip.

Her heart kept up its staccato rhythm, and Kate's knuckles were white as they gripped the steering wheel. Within less than fifteen minutes, the Pine Ridge city limits came into view. She made the turn toward the hospital and slowed to thirty-five miles per hour.

"Lord, please stop the bleeding," Kate murmured as she tapped her thumbs against the steering wheel. "Please let her be okay."

She pulled into the parking lot and rushed into the ER's waiting room. There were several people sitting in the padded chairs across from the check-in desk—an elderly couple, a woman with two small children, and a teenage boy. Kate hurried to talk to the heavyset woman behind the counter.

"Excuse me," Kate said. "I'm looking for a girl who just

came in, maybe half an hour ago. She was afraid she's having a miscarriage."

The receptionist glanced down at the paperwork on her desk, shuffling through and scanning the pages. Finally she looked back at Kate. "I'm sorry, but we haven't had anyone like that in here today."

Kate couldn't take in the woman's words at first. She stared at her. "Are you sure?"

The woman nodded. "I'm sorry. Is it a friend of yours?"

"Yes," Kate said as her mind turned to where Mouse could've gone. If not the ER, then where? Finally it came to her. She patted a hand on the counter just once, then moved quickly out the door, making her way to her car and then to the clinic across town.

The receptionist there was the same young man Kate had spoken with before. His expression when Kate came in the door said that he knew exactly who she was.

"Is she here?" Kate breathed.

"The girl you were looking for before?" He shook his head. "She left five minutes ago."

Kate glanced toward the door, hoping for a glimpse.

"Did she say where she was going?"

"No."

Then she turned back to the man. "Were they able to stop the bleeding?"

"Yes. But that doesn't mean she's out of the woods yet."

Kate returned to the parking lot. No one was there, save a few spring birds playing among the tall elm trees that lined the neighborhood street.

Kate glanced up and down the street. She'd missed her. By five short minutes, she'd missed her.

Had it been Marlee? Doubt edged in. The girl was too young to have her driver's license. If she was Mouse, how would she have gotten to the clinic? The message hadn't said how she planned on getting there. Perhaps someone had driven her. But if so, who?

Chapter Thirteen

When Kate got home, she went straight to her computer, which was still connected to the Internet in Paul's study.

A single line from Mouse was in Kate's e-mail: *They stopped the bleeding—the baby is okay.*

To have such a scare so early in the pregnancy couldn't be good. Had the doctor put the girl on bed rest? Was she at risk for more such episodes? The receptionist at the clinic seemed to think so. Mouse needed to tell her parents what was going on, for the sake of the child growing inside her.

Finally Kate sent her another message:

Dear Mouse,

> *I tried to find you today at the clinic. I missed you by a few minutes. I'm worried about you and about your baby. Did the doctor give you any special instructions? Please take good care of yourself.*

> *When you feel ready to tell me who you are, I want you to know that I won't betray your confidence. I won't*

tell anyone without your permission, but I will be here to encourage you and tell you that everything WILL be all right.

God is in the business of taking bad situations and turning them into something more amazing and wonderful than you could ever imagine. Hang on to that, okay?

Your friend,
Kate

The next Sunday at youth group, Kate was more than ready to talk to Marlee. What exactly she would say, Kate didn't know. How did one go about asking a teenage girl if she was pregnant? Her thoughts flicked to Livvy's reaction when she'd asked about Anne and James. And Livvy was a dear friend!

Kate watched the girl as she talked with her friends, trying to determine if there were any prompts for starting the conversation. Marlee looked tired, and when Paul started teaching on 1 Corinthians 13, she'd even fallen asleep.

"Hey, Miss Snores, wake up," Justin Jenner had teased.

She lifted bleary eyes. Dried drool covered one cheek. Everyone got a chuckle out of it, including Marlee.

"Marlee, do you have a minute?" Kate said once the teens started to amble off toward home.

The teenager nodded and turned toward her, arms crossed over her midsection. She waved good-bye to Brenna, then gave Kate her full attention.

"You okay?" Kate asked.

Marlee shrugged her shoulders and looked away. Kate

could see the unshed tears welling in her eyes. This was the second Sunday in a row where the girl was visibly upset.

"What's wrong?"

"There's nothing to tell," Marlee said. "I'm fine."

"Are you sure? I want you to know you can talk to me if there's something going on. Did you see my message to everyone on FriendsForever?"

The girl shook her head even as tears began to trace her freckled cheeks.

"I stopped by the cemetery the other day," Kate began, careful to watch the girl's expression, "and visited your mother's grave."

Marlee looked at her, her brow furrowed. "Why are you telling me this?"

"Her headstone has a Celtic cross on it."

"We're Welsh. So ... ?"

Either Marlee was an excellent actress, or she had no idea what Kate was talking about.

"Is there anything else? My dad's probably waiting in the parking lot. He doesn't like it when I make him wait."

"Of course," Kate said. "You head on home. But Marlee." The girl met her gaze. "Let me know if there's anything you need to talk about, okay?"

Marlee merely shrugged again and then she was out the door.

Perhaps Marlee wasn't the girl after all. Doubt began to edge in, though Kate knew, based on her conversation with Brenna, that something was amiss in Marlee's life, even if she wasn't Mouse. And Kate couldn't get past the blank expression on Marlee's face when she'd asked about the Celtic cross. Did that mean Marlee had nothing to do with the letter or that Kate was making more of the Celtic cross than was justified? Yet Brenna's comment that Marlee was close to her father seemed important too. A teen who was close to her father would be more concerned about disappointing him than a teen who wasn't.

WHEN KATE AND PAUL got home from youth group, it was almost nine o'clock.

"Hey," Paul said, "the guys and I were talking about heading out on an overnight fishing excursion on the eighteenth. It's a Friday night. We'd be back Saturday afternoon. Does that work for you?"

"Um . . ." Kate hesitated.

The eighteenth was a little less than two weeks away. Kate hadn't thought through what was on her schedule for the next day much less that far out, yet there was something about the eighteenth that stuck in her brain. What was it?

Finally, when she couldn't recall what it was, she said, "The eighteenth is fine."

BEFORE BED, Kate sat down at her laptop in the kitchen and composed her next e-mail to Mouse:

Dear Mouse,

I don't know if you can tell that I'm praying for you and that I'm concerned about you. I hope so. I've been thinking of you constantly, especially after your scare.

How are you feeling? Have you told anyone? Did someone take you to the hospital? I don't want to intrude. I ask these questions out of concern for your well-being—and your baby.

Prayerfully,
Kate

Kate sent the message, then she went to Mouse's home page. Nothing new had been posted. No added Friends, just Kate and that same picture of a mouse. Kate moved back to her own page and saw that there was a note on her bulletin board from Ronda at the beauty salon.

Dear Mrs. Hanlon,

I just saw that you had invited me to be your friend, so I thought I'd say hello.

Ronda

Kate glanced over the young beautician's home page. She had a total of 148 friends listed, most of them people from town, though there were plenty that said "from school" under the How I Know This Person tab.

Her favorite TV shows were the popular reality shows, as well as anything to do with makeovers and fashion, which, when Kate thought about it, made sense, considering that Ronda was a hair stylist. One show in particular stood out. The comment read, "I can't get enough of *Fashionista* on the Fashion Channel."

Kate had heard some of the kids at youth group talking

about the show too. She clicked over to Marlee's home page and glanced down the teen's list of favorite TV shows. It too listed *Fashionista* as her all-time favorite show.

From what Kate could tell, the TV show was a contest among fashion designers in which someone was eliminated every week, and the winner received a large sum of cash to help start up a signature clothing line.

"I can't wait to see who wins," Marlee had posted on her bulletin board. "I hope it isn't that weird guy, Lemuel."

Brenna had responded, "Come on, M! Lemuel is the BEST."

As Kate read, an idea came to her. She could host a season-finale party for the show. She could even make it a sleepover. They could watch the show together, maybe even do a makeover or two. If Kate could convince Ronda to come, they could have fun with new hairstyles.

She checked out the schedule for the show and saw that the finale was Friday the eighteenth. Wasn't that the day Paul had scheduled his fishing trip?

That was when she remembered . . . April eighteenth was the anniversary of their first date. In all their years, they'd always celebrated it together.

How could she have forgotten?

She went to find Paul, who was in his study.

"Hey," she said. Paul lifted his head from his reading to look at her. "Did you say that you wanted to go fishing on Friday the eighteenth?"

Paul nodded. "Yeah. It's the opener. There's a lake outside of Saint Thomas that Danny says has the best bass."

She studied him for a long moment. He'd never forgotten the date before. Perhaps he was planning a surprise for her. She decided to let it go. It wasn't as if they couldn't make other plans to celebrate the day. Besides, if he was gone, it would be easier to plan a party for the girls.

"I'm going to plan a girls' sleepover here, then, on that night . . . unless there are scheduling conflicts."

"Sounds good to me."

She glanced at him as he returned to his reading.

Was he playing coy, or had he truly forgotten? She tried to shake it off, yet she was disappointed.

Well, she decided, perhaps this was just the opportunity she was looking for to get to know the girls better. She would focus on that instead. She returned to the kitchen and began to compose the invitation she would post on her FriendsForever bulletin board.

Girls Only, it said. *Come to my house Friday the eighteenth at six thirty to watch the season finale of* Fashionista *on the Fashion Channel. Wear your most prize-worthy outfit, purchased or made yourself, and we'll award prizes for the most creative, most wearable, and most trendy. And bring your pj's and sleeping bag to stay for a sleepover. Feel free to invite your friends; the more the merrier.*

Hope to see you then.

Kate

Chapter Fourteen

Kate's slippers made a whispering sound as she moved around the cheery kitchen the next morning making breakfast after her morning devotions. The small kitchen had faded yellow cupboards and copper pots that hung from a rack on the ceiling. She grabbed one of the pans and set it on the ancient stove, then pulled a carton of eggs from the refrigerator.

Paul was at the dining table. His small tackle box was open before him, with lures, sinkers and bobbers lined up across the wooden surface.

"What are you up to?" she asked as she whisked the eggs.

Paul lifted his head. "Sorting. Organizing."

"Are you going fishing again?" Kate glanced at the well-worn fishing box.

"Eventually," he said. "Danny mentioned going again on Saturday."

"This Saturday *and* the eighteenth?"

Paul shrugged. "We're having fun."

Kate smiled at him despite the twinge in her stomach. The kitchen was silent for a few moments. "Breakfast is ready."

She got the salt and pepper shakers down from the cupboard and placed them on the kitchen counter while Paul put his gear away and wiped the table with a clean rag. Then she poured two glasses of cold milk and Paul helped her set the table.

Finally they sat and bowed their heads to pray. Then Paul took a bite of his omelet.

"Mmm. Good stuff, Katie." He paused. "Oh, I forgot to tell you. Carl Wilson called for you yesterday."

"Oh yeah?"

"He was looking for you; had some questions about the booths for the afterprom party." Paul took another bite of his omelet.

"And ... ?" Kate said.

"We got to talking, and it turns out he's taking a mechanics class at the vo-tech in Chattanooga."

"Did you ask if he and Ashley Williams are dating?"

"How could I just blurt that out? 'Are you dating Ashley Williams? Maybe having a baby with her?' Seemed too awkward to me." He took a swig of his milk. "Though when I think back, I wonder if you're onto something."

"What makes you say that?" The cheese-filled omelet tasted especially good to Kate, with just enough onion to give it punch.

"Do you remember when I'd gone over to help Carl with cutting some wood? It was a couple months back, and Scout had gotten in the way."

Kate recalled the incident.

Paul went on. "The dog got his tail cut, so we rushed him over to see the vet. It hadn't really seemed like much at the time, but now that I'm thinking back on it, Ashley did seem quite attentive, and Carl seemed to like her admiration. She hovered over that dog, but I didn't get the feeling it was because of the dog. You know what I mean? It was just the way Ashley looked at Carl."

THROUGHOUT THE DAY, Kate thought about what Paul had said about Carl. Sure, he was a nice young man. But nice young men made mistakes too.

When she finished her housework, she made her way to the washer and dryer area, which always seemed to be heaped with more loads to do than she had time for.

Her cell phone buzzed to life in her purse, and she rushed to answer it. When she glanced at the caller ID, she saw that it was Brenna Phillips. She glanced at her watch as she hit the Talk button. It was two thirty.

"Brenna?" Kate said.

The sound on the other end was human, though there were no decipherable words in the mix. The girl was sobbing and gulping big breaths of air as she spoke.

"Brenna, I'm not getting any of this," Kate said. "What's going on? Are you okay?"

"It's Marlee. She didn't show up for choir, so I called her on my cell between classes. She hung up on me."

Kate was puzzled. Didn't teenagers act that way all the time? Drama-queen scenes followed by apologies and forgotten misdeeds?

"Did you have an argument?" Kate asked.

"No. It wasn't like that . . ." She inhaled, and Kate took the opportunity to speak.

"Is she okay?"

"I don't know. She's never been this upset."

Kate's pulse quickened as worry edged up. If Marlee was Mouse, had she started spotting again?

"School's out in half an hour," Kate said. "How about if I pick you up? We can go to Marlee's together."

"Okay," Brenna gulped.

Kate heard her take a deep breath as if she was trying to calm herself.

"When did you talk to her?"

"A few minutes ago." She sobbed. "She was going on about her grandmother."

"I'll see you in a few, okay?"

Brenna agreed, and Kate pressed the End button on the phone.

"She was going on about her grandmother." The comment struck Kate, and with it a collection of other comments and observations. The nursing-home receptionist had said that Sarah Jones was "much better now." *Now?* So what had happened before, when she wasn't better? Dots began to connect. Marlee's moodiness, her close relationship with her grandmother . . .

Kate headed to her Honda, and within seconds the engine rumbled to life. She made her way down Smoky Mountain Road toward the high school, her thoughts untangling. Marlee hadn't muttered something about herself, hadn't told Brenna she was bleeding. She'd mentioned her grandmother. Just how long had the woman been in the nursing home? Kate hadn't thought to ask that. But as each realization came to her, she began to conclude that Marlee wasn't Mouse. But she was still a girl with heavy burdens to bear.

She maneuvered the car into the school's parking lot where buses and cars jockeyed toward the exits. Brenna was out front, so Kate pulled up to the curb and the girl got in.

"Thank you so much for doing this," Brenna said as she slid her backpack off and set it on the floor at her feet.

"I'm glad you called me," Kate said as she pulled in the line of cars aimed at the main street.

The girl looked anxiously through the windshield as she directed Kate to Marlee's house. She wrung her hands together like someone waiting for terrible news.

When they arrived at the Jones's bungalow-style house on Hamilton Road, Kate put the gearshift into park and killed the engine. The miniblinds were drawn tight against the day's sunshine. Kate walked up to the front porch. There was no doorbell, so she knocked on the door. No one answered. She tried to peek through the miniblinds, but all she could see was darkness.

"No one's answering the door," she told Brenna.

Brenna opened the screen door and knocked loudly on the wooden front door.

No sounds emanated from inside. She knocked harder. Still no answer. A short moment later, a car pulled into the driveway. A man climbed out of a Chevy pickup and looked at Kate and Brenna.

"Mr. Jones?" Kate said, walking toward him. He nodded and smiled, revealing even, straight teeth. He was a young, good-looking man with dark, close-cut hair, graying just at the temples, a dimple in his clean-shaven chin and chocolate-brown eyes.

"This is Mrs. Hanlon," Brenna offered, pointing to Kate. "She leads the youth group." The two shook hands.

"What's going on?" he said, his gaze turning to Brenna, whose face was still red from crying.

"I talked to Marlee on the phone. She was so upset. I was afraid . . ."

Marlee's dad turned to the house and unlocked the door. Kate and Brenna followed close behind. All was quiet except for the sound of a ticking clock and their footfalls.

"Marlee," her dad called, setting his keys on the hall table and moving to the stairs. "Marlee," his voice rose as he took the stairs two at a time.

Kate and Brenna followed, though at a distance. He threw Marlee's bedroom door open, and there she was, bawling her eyes out.

She lifted her red eyes to her father, and he knelt down alongside her bed. "What happened?"

"It's Grandma," she began, swiping at the wetness on her cheeks. "I called the nursing home after math. I wanted to tell Grandma that I got an A on that test I was worried about, and the nurse said that she had another stroke. They said they had tried to call you. I tried you too but you didn't pick up. I just couldn't stay in school anymore—"

She erupted in tears again, and her father swept her into his arms as if she were a little girl instead of a big teenager. When Marlee sat back on the bed, he looked at his cell phone. His face fell.

"My phone was on silent." He dialed a number and turned his back.

Kate moved next to Marlee and held her hand with Brenna on the other side, holding her while they watched him. The girl reached for a tissue on the nightstand by her bed and blew her nose loudly.

"This is David Jones. I'm calling about my mother." He inhaled loudly. "Oh no," he said. "What time?" There was a pause after each question. "Do I need to call the— Oh, okay. I'll call him then. Thank you."

When he turned toward them, the expression on his face said it all. "Marlee, honey. Grandma . . . just died."

Marlee's tears returned full force, and Brenna wrapped her arms around her friend.

"I knew something like this was going to happen," Marlee wailed.

Kate stroked the girl's hair, then she looked at Marlee's father and moved to a chair so he could comfort her. David sat on the floral-print bedspread next to Marlee. He was clearly in shock. He shook his head as if he couldn't believe what was happening.

"I guess I'll need to talk to someone about a funeral," he said.

"Do you have a church home?" Kate asked.

He shook his head. "But she went to Faith Community, so I suppose they should bury her."

Tears coursed down his cheeks. Kate's heart broke for the father and daughter. The teenager sobbed and sobbed as Brenna patted Marlee's hand.

"Do you have any family you need to call?" Kate asked.

David shook his head. "No, it was just us and Mom." He gazed tenderly at his daughter. "We thought she was going to pull out of it, come back home. Marlee's been beside herself with worry."

He reached for his daughter's hand and grasped it tightly. "Ever since my wife died, Marlee and my mom have been really close."

"It's like losing Mom all over again," Marlee moaned.

KATE SAT WITH THE JONESES for over an hour, consoling and comforting as he called co-workers and friends of his mother's. Finally David called the pastor at Faith Community and the funeral home in Pine Ridge. Both agreed to meet with the man to make all the proper arrangements the following morning.

Kate thought about canceling their counseling session with the Lewises that night, but when friends began to arrive at the Jones's home to offer their support and encouragement, she thought better of it.

Kate took her leave reluctantly.

"Thank you for coming," David said as he walked Kate to her car.

"It's the least I could do," Kate insisted.

Chapter Fifteen

Chad Lewis sat on the farthest end of the couch, so far from his wife that he looked as if he were trying to climb straight through the cushioned arm. After seeing the grief that the Joneses were suffering, his childishness almost made Kate angry, yet she knew that his actions stemmed from his own hurts and rejections. Her heart went out to him.

"Chad's been busy all week," Kim was saying. "When I do see him, he doesn't want to talk."

Chad leaned forward and rested his forearms on his knees as he spoke. "Kim doesn't seem to understand that this is the busy part of the year for me. Even taking off to come to these sessions is difficult. I simply have a lot of work right now."

Kate glanced at Kim as silent tears streamed down her cheeks. Chad followed Kate's gaze and then threw up his hands when he saw his wife.

"You see," he said, "I can't win. I make my living preparing tax returns, and it's April. It's no different than a farmer working the fields during harvest. My job comes with busy times and lax times. It's not like I can run off to Rock City like we used to. I have responsibilities!"

"Is that why you're crying, Kim?" Paul asked quietly.

Kim shook her head. "No." She paused for a moment, then sat up straighter. "I understand that Chad has to work harder at tax time. I get that." She looked at her husband. "It's about how he treats me. He thinks being busy means he can ignore me completely when he's home. I don't know why we thought we'd ever make good parents. We're a total mess."

"I don't ignore you."

"Kim . . . Chad,"—Kate kept her tone calm as her eyes met Paul's—"here's what I'm hearing. You tell me if I'm right."

She went on. "I'm hearing that you really miss your husband, Kim, especially during tax season, and that you, Chad, hope for more understanding from your wife because you're so busy and tired." She looked first at Kim and then at Chad. "Is that right?"

"I suppose," Chad conceded.

"Do you understand that Kim misses you?" Kate asked, wanting to get more out of the young man.

He folded his hands in front of him. Finally he said, "Of course I know that she misses me. But when we're together, all we talk about is how much she wants a baby, and I feel . . ." His words trailed away, and he sighed.

"Not talking about it won't bring us any resolution," Kim said.

Paul lifted his hands to stop them from saying more. "Did you complete your assignment?" he asked.

Kim nodded and pulled a sheet of paper from her purse, which was resting on the floor. She went to hand it to Paul, but he said, "No, read it to us."

She glanced at her husband before speaking, then began: "Rules for arguing: (1) Always show respect and love for each other; (2) No interrupting; (3) No name-calling; (4) No changing the subject; (5) Always listen, even if it's painful; (6) Be willing to look at yourself; don't point the finger back at the other person; (7) Don't go to bed angry; (8) Pray for each other every day; and (9) Offer one word of praise to each other daily."

She raised her head, waiting for Kate and Paul's response. "I would add a couple things," Paul suggested. "For listening, I would add something about looking for the real meaning behind what the other person is saying. And also, always assume the best."

Chad's brows knit together in obvious confusion.

Paul clarified, "To the core, Kim loves you. That guides her. That's what I mean by assuming the best. She wants to be close to you and be loved by you. That's her motive, though it doesn't always come out that way when she speaks."

Chad's face softened, and he took a deep breath. "It's my motive too," he said, turning toward her on the couch.

Kim began to sob. Chad pulled her to him and held her in his arms.

"I'm sorry I'm so insecure," she said.

"I'm sorry I'm not more sensitive to your needs," he answered.

Kate knew it was a big step.

When the session neared its end, Kim and Chad seemed to have crossed the invisible barrier that had held them apart. They even held hands as Paul gave them their assignment for the following week.

Kate brought out the snack and each straightened and reached for the plates Kate had set on the coffee table earlier. Their tears had dried, replaced by calm.

"That looks delicious, Mrs. Hanlon," Chad said, pointing to the hot cinnamon rolls on the platter.

Kate smiled at the young man, offering to serve him one of the large rolls.

When everyone had their snack in hand and was enjoying the taste of sugar and cinnamon, Paul said, "There's something else I'd like you to consider, especially now that tax season is almost over." He looked at Chad. "And that is finding healthy outlets. When we focus too much on ourselves, it's easy to get depressed and feel sorry for ourselves. We start to nitpick at our partners because we think if only they would change, we'd be happy. But that isn't where happiness comes from. Happiness is a by-product of a life lived for God. That's why the Bible says that to find our lives, we must lose them."

He looked at Kim, kindness in his blue eyes. "I'm talking about taking a break from trying to have a baby and using this time to do an activity, such as volunteering. There's nothing like reaching out to others to put life in perspective."

Kim turned to look at her husband. "I would be willing to do something like that."

"After next week, I'll have time again," Chad said.

"What do you suggest?" Kim asked.

"It depends on your interests," Paul said. "You could visit the nursing home in Pine Ridge or do fund-raising for charitable causes. Volunteer at the library . . ."

"The afterprom committee could use a young, vibrant couple like you to help out with our car-wash fund-raiser on Friday," Kate chimed in. "Or perhaps you could help out with the Faith Freezer Program. I'll be there cooking next week if you'd like to come. Also, we're looking for someone, or a couple, to take over the youth group."

"That's quite a list." Kim laughed.

"The point is," Paul said gently, "if God isn't going to give you a baby, you still have to live your lives, and he has a very good plan for you."

Kim's eyes clouded, and Kate knew she was considering what her future would be like without children. "Can we pray for you?" Paul asked.

Kim nodded.

"Dear heavenly Father," he began, "you know our needs and desires better than anyone. You know what makes us happy, and you want good things for us—good marriages that support us through life. Please teach Kim and Chad to listen to each other and truly hear. Teach them to be content, knowing that you love them."

KATE CLEARED THE DISHES from the coffee table after the Lewises had gone, then went into the kitchen to wash them up. The sudsy water felt warm against her hands; there was something comforting about it. Paul set a plate on the counter next to the sink and pulled her to him. Kate leaned her back against his chest as he wrapped his arms around her waist. She closed her eyes, enjoying the moment.

"I feel so bad for them," she finally said.

"God isn't going to let them go," Paul whispered to her neck.

She felt his warm breath on her skin and she turned to hug him. "I know you're right. I hope so."

She breathed deeply and moved back to the sink as Paul reached for a dishtowel.

"Do you wonder if they would be having these struggles if they'd been able to have children off the bat?" Kate asked.

"It's hard to say. They could be just fine, or they'd have kids *and* these problems."

"I suppose . . ." She wiped a plate and set it carefully in the rinse water.

"Every marriage has its struggles," Paul said. "For some couples, it's about finances, and for others, it's personality conflicts or different philosophies for child rearing."

"So what are our struggles?" She tilted her head toward him, teasing him.

"Besides the constant temptation I experience because of your baking? Other than that, I think we're doing pretty well."

Kate laughed.

"And you still laugh at my jokes," he said.

"You still surprise me with your wisdom." Kate's tone turned serious.

"I do?"

"All the time. You're a man who loves God, and it comes through in all you do."

WHEN PAUL WENT into the bathroom to get ready for bed, Kate tugged the bed covers up, pulled out the Bible she kept in her nightstand, and turned to Psalm 139. She needed to think, to pray, for Marlee and David Jones, for Mouse and her unborn baby, and for Kim and Chad Lewis. Her heart was heavy for all of them.

As she read, the words seemed to speak directly to her.

You created my inmost being;
you knit me together in my mother's womb. . . .

She paused to pray for Mouse—that she would know in her heart that those words were true, that God was knitting her child together. God had a plan for her baby.

Kate closed her eyes, allowing the passage to sink in. She'd been praying for Mouse and her child, but as she continued to pray, the image of Kim and Chad Lewis came unbidden. Then the two prayers melded as one. Kate's eyes flew open.

Was that what God had intended all along? Why hadn't she seen it earlier?

"MOUSE'S BABY COULD BE the answer to Kim and Chad's prayers," Kate told Paul when he came out of the bathroom.

Paul turned to look at her. His eyes shone with love. "That's an interesting idea, Katie. And I know you want to help this girl and the Lewises, but I'm not sure Chad and Kim are ready to have a baby . . ."

He shook his head as he removed his slippers and climbed into bed. "I mean, they were considering separating not that long ago. They may need more healing in their marriage before exploring any ideas about adoption."

"But, if I could just tell them about Mouse . . ."

"I'm not sure you should tell the Lewises about Mouse," Paul said, shaking his head again.

"Why not?"

"You don't even know who this girl is yet. You don't know if she wants to keep her baby or place it for adoption. That's not an easy thing for a mother to do."

Kate sat back. The very thought of giving one of her own children to another family told her Paul was right.

"I know you care," Paul said, touching her hand, "but God is going to have to work out the details, both for Mouse and in the Lewises' marriage."

"So, you think it's possible?"

"All things are possible." He gave her a lopsided grin.

LORD, KATE PRAYED silently as she lay in bed with Paul asleep beside her, *you know what's best for everyone—the Lewises, Mouse, her baby. Work your will in their lives and help me to hold the future with an open hand. Help me rely on you, trusting that you love each of these people and will work things for their best.*

And yet she wished that things would work out somehow,

that Kim and Chad could have a child to adore, that Mouse could find the answers to her problems while knowing that she'd done the right thing.

But most of all, Kate prayed that this baby who was coming into the world would arrive knowing that he or she was loved and wanted, as all children should be.

Chapter Sixteen

Kate's hair appointment at Betty's was set for three o'clock Tuesday afternoon. She sat on the padded vinyl bench by the front door and stared absently at the white and aqua checkerboard pattern of the floor tiles. The scent of perm solution was particularly strong, as three elderly women sat with tiny curlers in their gray hair, waiting the requisite time for the chemical to do its magic.

Betty was chatting with one of the women, while Ronda was at the shampooing station in the back. Kate could just make her out as she moved in and out of view from behind the partition.

A few minutes later, Ronda and a woman emerged. The woman's hair was wet and tightly curled, further evidence of the perm solution that scented the air. Ronda asked her if she'd like her hair styled, which the woman declined, so they moved to the front to finish their business.

Kate met Ronda's bloodshot eyes. The circles under them attested to a deep need for sleep. Ronda took the woman's check and tapped her pen on the appointment book while the woman looked through a little calendar she pulled from her purse.

Ronda was a medium-sized girl, not too large, yet not petite either. Her brown hair had auburn highlights, and her eyes were more amber than brown.

When the woman left, Ronda disappeared to the back for a few minutes. Kate assumed she was cleaning up before calling Kate over. Then she returned and waved Kate to an empty chair.

"So, what did you have in mind today, Mrs. Hanlon?" Ronda said as she touched her hair and looked at her in the mirror.

Kate caught Betty's glance and hoped she wasn't offended that she'd asked for the young stylist instead of her. She winked at Kate.

"Just a trim please."

"You should change your style," Betty said as Ronda brushed through Kate's hair. "There's nothing like a change in hairstyles to boost a person's self-esteem."

Kate was all too aware of Betty's makeover reputation. Sometimes the makeovers went well; sometimes they didn't.

"How about some highlights? You'd look great with a little honey color right by your face," Betty suggested.

Kate started to say no and then decided it wouldn't hurt to try something new. Besides, it would give her more time to talk to Ronda.

"Say," Kate changed the subject, looking toward Betty, "did you ever figure out who sent the flowers?"

Betty shook her head, pointing to the bouquet that was

sitting on the counter at the front of the shop. While the flowers were beginning to wilt, the arrangement still held most of its charm.

"Can I see the card again?" Kate asked, and Betty retrieved it from the daisies' midst. Kate read the words again. "To a woman who inspires me. I've admired you for a long, long time."

"I think it has to be someone you know well," Kate said. "Did you call the florist and ask who the sender was?"

"Nope, didn't even think of it. I'll do that." Betty turned her attention back to her customer.

When Kate looked in the mirror at Ronda, she saw that the young woman had gone pale.

"Are you okay?" Kate asked.

"I'm fine." Ronda waved it off. "I don't react well to the smell of the perm solution, and today . . ." She waved her hand to indicate the customers who were to blame, though she didn't say as much. "I'll be okay in a minute."

She sat in one of the chairs under the hairdryers and placed her head in her hands. Kate watched her, wishing she could read the young woman's mind. After a few long moments, Ronda stood and excused herself to mix up the dye for Kate's color job.

When she returned, she looked slightly improved.

"So," Kate began, wanting to get to the reason for her visit, other than the hair job. "Have you been feeling ill long?"

Ronda looked at her in the mirror. "It comes and goes."

"You think it's the perm solution?"

"I don't know what it is." She glanced at her boss, who was engrossed in conversation with her client. "Betty thinks

I'm nuts, that a person doesn't just develop a sensitivity to perm solution after so much time." She shrugged.

Kate studied Ronda's face in the mirror. She wore no makeup, save a little eyeliner on her top lid, and the auburn highlights in her brown hair seemed to match the hue of her eyes. Was she lying? The way she kept glancing at Betty seemed to indicate that she might be.

"Oh, I forgot something," Ronda said, excusing herself to go to the back again.

When she didn't return after a few minutes, Betty, who'd just brought her customer back from the shampooing sink, turned to Kate and began to talk.

"So," Betty said, "What have you been up to?"

Kate paused to think of an answer. She couldn't very well say, "I've been looking for a pregnant girl." So she said, "Regular stuff—mostly the afterprom party, planning youth-group events now that Max Wilcox is gone, and some couples' counseling. David Jones's mother passed away yesterday, so I'll be attending the funeral tomorrow."

"I'd heard about that. It's so sad," Betty said. She turned on a blow-dryer with a large diffuser attached to the end and fluffed her client's gray hair with her fingers as she dried.

Ronda returned and began to paint the foul-smelling dye mixture onto Kate's hair, starting at the roots and moving toward the ends. She worked quietly. Kate studied her weary-looking face in the mirror.

"What kinds of things do you and Paul deal with in your couples' counseling?" Betty asked, recapturing Kate's attention from the neighboring station.

Kate glanced at her, knowing that Betty was simply making small talk, yet Kate had wanted to talk to Ronda more.

"Most everything you can imagine," Kate said. "We're talking to one young couple about some fertility issues . . ."

She knew she couldn't go into detail, but as soon as she'd mentioned fertility issues, she noticed that Betty had stopped working and was staring at her.

"Did I say something wrong?" Kate said.

Betty shook her head. "Oh no, not at all. But did you know that Bob and I had problems in that area?"

Kate turned to her. "I had no idea."

Betty nodded gravely. "It about tore our marriage apart. The blame and guilt we felt. It was unbearable."

The pain of it could still be seen in her gray eyes as she spoke. "We first tried to have kids about two years after we got married." She resumed styling her customer's hair as she spoke, and the woman seemed intent on her story as well.

"Two months later, I was pregnant—no problem. We were so happy, and I started decorating our second bedroom and buying baby furniture. Then about five months in, I had a miscarriage."

She paused again and met Kate's eyes. "It was the worst feeling I've ever had, knowing that my baby wouldn't live." Her eyes clouded, and she fluttered a hand to her chest. "We tried again, but we had the same result every time. I had four miscarriages and it was more than I could bear. Bob felt like it was all his fault, and I thought it was mine." She shook her head. "It's a miracle our marriage survived it."

"But you have kids," Kate said, and Betty's face lit in a

giant smile. Kate was amazed at how willing Betty was to talk about her own experience with infertility.

"And that was another miracle," Betty said, "a miracle called adoption. We adopted George first, and then somehow I was able to carry my next pregnancy to term. The boys are only ten months apart."

"I've never heard you talk about this," Kate said, glancing at Ronda. Her head was down as if she were concentrating extra hard on her work, but Kate saw her eyes dart to Betty.

"I guess it's such a natural part of my life, I don't think to mention it. With the boys living so far away now, people around here tend to forget. George has always known, of course, since he was little when he was adopted."

"What are their names?" the customer under her care asked.

"George and John," Betty said. "The lights of my life."

"How long did it take you to adopt?" Kate asked.

"Your color just needs to set now," Ronda interrupted. "Do you mind if I go out back for a little bit while it sets?"

She was acting very jittery, and Kate studied her for a long moment as she busily cleaned up supplies. Finally Ronda said again, "You don't mind, do you?"

"Of course not. Are you okay?" Kate said.

"I'm fine," she said, but her body language said she couldn't get out of there soon enough. "I'll be back as soon as you're ready to rinse," Ronda promised.

"No problem."

Ronda disappeared into the back room.

"That girl," Betty said with a sigh. "You see what I mean?"

She shook her head. "Now, what were we talking about?" She moved to the other side of her client, backcombing and hair-spraying as she talked.

Kate wished she could follow Ronda to see if she could help, but with the solution on her hair and the shampoo cape around her and Betty still chatting, she wasn't exactly mobile. And Kate hadn't yet found an opening in the conversation to ask Ronda if she had a boyfriend. She'd have to find a way to steer the conversation in that direction when Ronda came back.

Betty chewed her bottom lip for a moment, then said, "The adoption took a little over a year, I guess. Though I was a bit worried we could still lose him."

"There was a chance the birth mother could've taken him back, right?" Betty's customer said.

Betty nodded.

"It happens," Betty agreed. "And yet it was so worth the risk."

There was a light in Betty's eyes as she spoke. It made her think of Kim Lewis and her sparkly personality. Though the timing might be difficult, the sense Kate had had the night before that God had a bigger plan in mind rang with a note of truth.

It wasn't until Betty had finished telling the story that Kate realized Ronda had been gone far too long. She glanced at her watch—she'd had the dye on her hair almost twice as long as she normally did.

She looked up in panic and said, pointing to her watch, "Betty, where's Ronda?"

Betty gasped and ran toward the back of the salon, then Kate saw her dart to the front door. A few moments later, a sickly looking Ronda returned, hustling to Kate. Her eyes were rimmed in red, and her cheeks were blotchy.

"I'm so sorry," she panted, motioning for Kate to head to the shampooing sink. "I wasn't feeling well, and I lost track of the time."

She leaned Kate back into the sink and quickly rinsed her hair with warm water. Then Ronda lifted Kate upright and began to towel dry her locks.

"Oh no," Kate heard the stylist utter under her breath.

"What is it?" Kate said, knowing full well that hair dye left on that long was bound to have an unpleasant effect.

Ronda's brow furrowed as she handed Kate a mirror. Kate gazed at her reflection, and what she saw wasn't a middle-aged woman with medium strawberry blonde hair. Instead, she looked like a pale lion with a blazing sun for a mane. Her mouth dropped open in horror.

"My hair is orange," she gasped.

Betty must have heard her despite the partition that separated the shampooing station from the rest of the salon, because suddenly she was right there.

"Oh my," she sputtered, turning to Ronda. "How could you have left her? You knew what would happen."

"I didn't mean to." Ronda looked mortified, and Kate felt horrible.

"It's okay," Kate soothed, patting the girl's hand.

"I'll redye if for you, Kate," Betty insisted. "Can you stay longer? I'm sure I can make room in the schedule."

Kate glanced at her watch. It was already four thirty. She had an afterprom meeting scheduled for five o'clock, not nearly enough time to redye her hair.

"I have a meeting, so I'll leave it as it is," Kate said.

"You didn't even get your hair cut yet," Betty said.

Kate shrugged, hating the idea of going out in public like that. In a town the size of Copper Mill, a flame-colored mane was bound to start rumors.

"Well, tomorrow, then?" Betty said. "I just feel awful."

Kate rose and took off the cape that encompassed her, handing it and the mirror to Betty, then she reached for her handbag.

"It's all right. I'll give you a call tomorrow."

"I'll make this up to you, Kate," Betty insisted.

Kate patted Betty's shoulder and gave Ronda a reassuring look. "Really, it'll be okay."

Chapter Seventeen

By the time Kate arrived at the afterprom meeting, she'd all but forgotten about her hair. The uncomfortable stares of the other committee members soon reminded her.

"Kate"—it was Livvy Jenner—"what happened to your hair?"

"Oh." Kate touched her pumpkin-colored locks. "It's a long story."

Livvy raised an eyebrow.

"Ronda was a bit distracted," she said.

"So this is her doing?"

"*Mm-hmm*," Kate said. "She was nauseous most of the appointment."

"She was?"

Kate thought of how Ronda had left in the middle of Betty's story of infertility and adoption. Had the emotion of Betty's story been too much for the girl to bear? Kate had seen her red-rimmed eyes and the blotchy look of her skin.

Ashley Williams came in just then. She looked much better than the last time Kate had seen her. Her cheeks had a rosy glow, and her green eyes shone with what looked like joy. Kate caught her eye, and she came over to join her and Livvy.

"I'm glad you could make it, Ashley," Kate said, extending a hug to the dark-haired girl.

"Thanks for inviting me," Ashley said as her eyes edged up to Kate's head. She said nothing about the blaze of color.

"You'll have to let me know what you want to do. We have a car wash and party decor, and there's always booth painting . . . ," Kate said, grateful that Ashley didn't mention her new do.

"I'm not too fussy." Ashley shrugged. "I'll do whatever you need."

Just then, Carl Wilson joined the other mingling committee members. Kate watched Ashley to see if she would notice him. When she did, her eyes widened, and her breathing seemed to quicken.

"Carl," Ashley whispered.

Kate's eyes met Livvy's. Then she glanced at the tall, lean, blond man, then back at Ashley. The young woman's gaze was intent on him, and Kate could sense that she longed to go speak to him.

"Let's go have a seat and get our meeting started," Kate said.

Ashley turned back to Kate and gave her a sweet smile as if she was glad for the change in topic.

Angie Petzel and Anne Jackson showed up too. Angie was in her usual creative garb. This outfit was a pair of wild-printed bell-bottoms topped with a T-shirt that seemed too worn out to be called clothing and a long tunic that reached almost to the girl's knees, accentuating her thin frame. She and Anne found James Jenner in the back and sat with him.

Angie waved shyly as Kate moved to start the meeting. She pointed to her own hair, indicating Kate's new look, and then gave her a thumbs-up. Kate blushed and smiled at her.

"Let's gather round," Kate said, taking in the crowd from the front as people took their seats. When the chitchat died down, she added, "I'm so glad to see more youth groupers here tonight. I know that your valuable input will help us make a better afterprom party, and it will encourage your friends at school to join in the fun."

Kate moved to the topic of painting the booths and mentioned that they were still waiting for the lumber because of a mix-up at the lumberyard. When she asked about volunteers to help with the painting, Angie was the first to raise her hand.

"I'd like to help with those," the girl said. "I like to paint."

Kate nodded and said, "Thanks, Angie. Sounds great."

Kate wrote her name on a list of volunteers helping with that aspect of the preparations.

"The theme for the night is Under a Starry Sky. Carl will have a list of what each of the games will be."

Her gaze turned to the adults who had already come up with preliminary plans for each booth. "We'll make eight booths, so it'll take some doing. Carl Wilson and Joe Tucker will be building them." She turned to Carl and said, "Any idea when the lumber will be here?"

"Should be soon. Or so they tell me," he said.

Kate saw his gaze move briefly to Ashley.

Kate looked back to Angie. "Carl can give you a call when they're ready to start."

"If I can paint after work," Angie said, "I think I can volunteer a few hours a week."

Kate understood how very difficult it was in this day and age to juggle the many, many aspects of life. She'd been running from one commitment to the next all week, and she felt ready for a good long nap. Teenagers these days had it worse. Most of them had jobs and plenty of homework to do each night, not to mention keeping up with the social aspects of their lives and sports.

"With prom a month and two days away, I think we'll be just fine on that front," Kate said.

Ashley's hand edged up. "I'd like to paint the booths too."

Kate smiled at her. "The more the merrier."

AFTER THE MEETING ADJOURNED, Kate watched Carl Wilson amble over to Ashley Williams on the other side of the room. Soon the two were engrossed in conversation. They stood a little too close, and Ashley's gaze was intent on his face.

Angie Petzel came up to Kate. Kate turned her attention to the girl.

"I like your hair," Angie said, pointing to the orange atrocity.

Kate laughed. "This hair is an accident."

"Well, it still looks hot," Angie insisted.

"You're sweet," Kate said.

"Hey, I saw your invite to the *Fashionista* party. I will totally be there."

"Oh, that's great. I saw on FriendsForever that a lot of the girls seem to like the show, so I thought it'd be a good excuse to get together."

Angie smiled. "There's nothing like a good excuse to hang out with the girls. And your invitation says a lot about how much you care."

ONCE KATE GOT HOME, she went to the bedroom and flipped open her laptop, plugging in the phone cord. After the several minutes it took to connect to the Internet, she clicked on the FriendsForever hyperlink. Dial-up was particularly slow, so she went to the kitchen to pull out food for supper. Kate glanced at her watch, wondering what was keeping Paul.

After she set a casserole in the oven to reheat, she checked her in-box. There were two messages: one from Angie Petzel and the other from Mouse. Kate's heart skipped a beat.

She quickly opened the message from the mysterious sender.

Dear Mrs. Hanlon,

I know you're looking out for me and praying for me. I can feel it. I saw how much you cared when you talked to me. Thank you for that.

I thought about what you said in your e-mail the other day. To be honest, it's pretty hard to believe that God cares about someone like me. My folks are very big into church, yet all I ever see from them is judgment. I'm constantly hearing how much I fail, how much I don't get right. Even when I do my very best, it isn't good enough for them.

That's why it'll devastate them when I have to break the news about the baby. I can't even think about that now. When I went to the doctor, I got to hear the baby's heartbeat. Part of me is amazed, but the rest, the part that has to live in the real world, is terrified.

I have to tell my boyfriend regardless of what it does

to our relationship. It tears me up to think about it. But the next time I see him, I'm going to do it. Pray that I won't lose my nerve.

Mouse

Kate stared at the words. She'd talked to this girl. Who could it be? She closed her eyes and prayed for Mouse. Then she began to type from the heart.

Dear Mouse,

Be assured that I am indeed praying for you and thinking of you as you get ready to break the news to your boyfriend. I know this can't be easy for you.

I've been giving your situation much thought, and you need to know that there is an option for you if you don't feel you can raise your baby yourself. Adoption is a wonderful and beautiful gift to couples who can't have children on their own. Many couples are longing for a baby of their own to love and care for.

There's a couple I know here in Copper Mill. She's a kindergarten teacher, and he's an accountant. They desperately want a baby, but they haven't been able to have one. They would be amazing parents.

I'm not saying that you must go this route, but it is something to consider and pray about.

Whatever you decide, know that I'm praying, and I'm always willing to discuss anything with you.

Your dear friend,
Kate

When Paul got home, he stood in the entryway staring at his wife. At first, Kate had no idea what was wrong. His mouth was agape, his eyes wide.

"What in the world?" he said. He pointed to the top of his own head.

Kate felt her strawlike locks, and memory returned.

"There was a little mishap at the salon."

He laughed. "Okay . . . I thought maybe you were trying to spice things up in our marriage."

"Why? Do you like this?" Kate placed her hands on her hips.

Paul's brow furrowed for a moment. "Let's just say there are better ways to be mysterious." He pulled her into his arms and gave her a kiss.

"Are you sure? Because this seems to be working pretty well!"

"Very funny." He smiled, then his face sobered.

"Did you get a chance to visit the Joneses?" Kate guessed at the cause of his mood change.

Paul nodded. "I stopped by the house. The pastor from Faith Community was there too—they were planning the funeral. Poor David and Marlee. They've been through so much already."

Chapter Eighteen

Mourners stared with empty, tear-filled gazes as the casket was lowered into the ground the following morning. Marlee clutched her father's hand tightly, and Brenna reached over to hug her. Kate wished she could comfort Marlee, yet she knew that only time and God's healing could truly accomplish that goal.

The small group of mourners moved off toward their cars and the lunch that awaited them at the church while Marlee and David Jones lingered at the grave site. Kate came up behind them, and Marlee turned to her. She swiped at her tear-stained face with a tissue.

"Thanks for being there on Monday," Marlee said. "I didn't know what to do."

"I'm glad I was there too. Your grandmother was lucky to have you, to be so close to you."

Marlee smiled, then closed her eyes. "I was the lucky one."

THAT AFTERNOON, Kate decided to take a walk around town. The day was splendid. Sunshine warmed the streets, and robins bopped from spot to spot on the greening grass. Kate inhaled, allowing spring to waft over her.

The lumber that Carl Wilson had ordered for the after-prom booths had been delivered to Carl's place around one thirty. He'd called to tell Kate of its arrival.

Kate drove to his place, and Joe Tucker arrived shortly thereafter. The older man inspected the order to make sure everything was accounted for and started in on building the booths right away.

When Kate had asked what she could do, Joe had promptly told her she wasn't needed, and she'd better stop trying to be Wonder Woman.

"You're making the rest of us look bad," he'd said with a wink.

Kate smiled at the recollection as she passed Emma's Ice Cream on Main Street. She looked up and saw Angie Petzel coming toward her on the sidewalk. The teen smiled when she saw Kate and gave a little wave.

"Are you headed to work?" Kate asked.

"Yeah."

Kate glanced at the girl's adorable outfit, this one a schoolgirl look with tartan plaid.

"Cute outfit," Kate said.

"Thanks. I design pretty much everything I wear."

"You made that?" Kate shook her head, amazed that someone so young could be so talented.

"I've been doing it forever," Angie said with a dismissive wave of her hand.

"You're definitely an artsy girl, Angie. It's impressive."

Angie blushed. "Thanks. I love doing creative things. It

gives me a sense of purpose, you know?" Her gaze lifted to Kate's hairdo.

Kate's cheeks warmed. "I have an appointment to change it back to my regular color."

"That's too bad," Angie said with a laugh. "You're someone who could really pull something like that off, you know?"

Kate wasn't sure what she meant though she felt vaguely complimented.

Angie went on, "I mean that you're really a confident person. It shows in how you carry yourself."

Kate studied the eighteen-year-old, who shrugged when she finished speaking. Kate knew she was completely sincere in the compliment.

"You carry yourself well too," Kate said.

Angie gave a slight shake of her head. "Looks can be deceiving."

"What do you mean?"

"Oh nothing . . ." She laughed and pushed a hand at the air as her words fell away.

"I was glad to see you at the meeting last night," Kate said. "Oh, and the lumber arrived this morning. Some of the men are starting construction on the booths today, and they should be ready to paint by tomorrow night. There are some others coming to paint then too, around six. I was going to call you, but since you're here . . ."

"That sounds perfect. I'll stop by after work, then. It sounded like there will be quite a paint crew. Will you be there?"

Kate heard the hopeful note in her voice. She felt glad the girl was becoming more than an acquaintance. She could be a good influence among the other girls with her confidence and drive.

"I'll be there," Kate said, then the two went their separate ways.

DID YOU TELL YOUR BOYFRIEND? Kate wrote that night on FriendsForever after choir practice, the images of Ronda and Ashley flashing in her mind as she typed. All day long, she'd been thinking about it, wondering how the boy took the news of his impending fatherhood. Had Mouse really gone through with it? Or had she chickened out?

Kate wished the girl was online right then so she wouldn't have to wait for an answer.

But there was no answer that night. Kate worried about what that meant.

"HEYA," RONDA SAID THE NEXT DAY as she entered the large Faith Briar fellowship hall, where several of the young people had gathered to begin painting the booths. Kate was surprised to see her there, considering she hadn't had a chance to talk to her about the event. She seemed in a better mood and she looked healthier.

"Ashley told me about tonight, so I thought I'd volunteer," she said. "I thought you'd be in today to get your hair fixed." Her gaze traveled to Kate's head.

"I have an appointment for next week," Kate said. "Alicia said you were booked."

"Oh . . . okay. Well, I'm so sorry about that."

Kate patted Ronda's hand and smiled into her eyes. Then

Ronda excused herself and waved at Ashley before making her way to the girl who was putting a primer coat on one of the wooden game booths that Carl and Joe had built. Ronda wasn't a Faith Briar regular, so Kate appreciated that the girl would so willingly give up her free time to help out.

Kate carried a paint brush to Ronda.

"So how long have you and Ashley been friends?" Kate asked, looking between the two.

Ashley Williams wore a tan cardigan with a khaki skirt and a white cotton blouse. It looked more like a Catholic-school uniform than something a girl her age would wear to a painting party. The buttons on her blouse bulged a little, attesting to the rumored weight gain.

"We graduated high school together, but we didn't really hang out much then. We've become better acquainted since our classmates left for college," Ashley said, glancing at Ronda. "She was one of the popular girls."

"I was not," Ronda said, taking the brush from Kate and chuckling. "I was the one with really big hair, remember?"

Ashley smiled and moved the paint bucket between them to share, and they were soon busy painting, using the sketches Angie had drawn up as a guide for the design. Kate ambled around the room, checking on everyone's progress and answering any questions that came up. Finally she got herself a cup of coffee. When she turned back toward the room, she saw Ashley and Angie chatting. At one point, Carl came by, and Ashley smiled up at him.

Kate waved at her, and the T-shirt-clad eighteen-year-old came over.

"What would you like me to do?" She stuffed her hands in her jeans pockets and looked around the busy room.

"You've already done a lot."

Kate referred to the drawings for each booth that Angie had left with Carl Wilson. The booths kept to the starry theme, with Jupiter, Saturn, and Mars all given equal space in the entourage while being bright and creative.

"Ashley and Ronda are painting the base coat on that booth," Kate pointed to the twosome. "Would you like to decorate one of the dry ones?" She motioned to the lineup of plain navy booths.

Kate led the teen to the collection of tempera paints on the kitchen counter. Angie gathered her needed supplies and soon was painting. Kate grabbed a brush and took up residence on the opposite side of the booth that Angie was working on.

"You paint, Mrs. Hanlon?" Angie asked.

"I love to draw and paint," Kate said. "I have a stained-glass studio in my house, so I draw designs for windows and lamps all the time."

Angie poked her head around the side and looked at her.

"Really?" she said. "I didn't know that about you."

"You'd be surprised what else you don't know," Kate said, raising a mysterious eyebrow.

There was something magnetic about Angie, Kate thought as they chatted. Maybe it was the sense of confidence she exuded, or the creativity that seemed to ooze from her very pores. It gave her an air of artistic flair.

"I have the perfect outfit to bring for your contest," Angie said.

"The *Fashionista* party?"

"Yup. You'd better have good prizes."

"Now I'm nervous," Kate laughed. "But I've got some good stuff planned."

They painted in comfortable silence for a while.

"What church do you attend again?" Kate finally asked. "You mentioned going somewhere in Pine Ridge?"

"Yeah," Angie said. "It's not the best, but I've been going there my whole life."

"Not the best . . . What do you mean?"

"If it was up to me, I'd go someplace closer to home, like Faith Briar, where I'm with the people from my own town. It's hard to feel connected over there." She shrugged and continued painting. "I don't really know those people. And they don't exactly reach out."

Kate looked at Angie. Her eyes were focused on her work, but there was obvious hurt in them. Kate wondered what had happened to cause it.

"So," Kate said, "tell me about your family."

"I have four sisters—Caitlin, Elizabeth, Amy, and Kris. They're all younger than me."

"That's a houseful," Kate said. "Are you close to each other?"

"I suppose. But lately we seem to argue a lot. My folks are really busy, though, so they don't seem to notice."

"What do you mean?"

Angie paused before going on. "My dad has a business here in town—they make catalogs for other companies—and mother . . . she's a stay-at-home mom."

Kate dipped her brush in the orange paint and continued to add stars to the navy background.

"She volunteers so much at church that half the time I don't see her. She's always running from one Bible study to the next. I kinda miss her."

Kate was just about to say more when Ronda shouted from the other side of the room, "Call an ambulance!"

Kate looked toward Ronda, and next to her lay Ashley in a heap on the floor.

Chapter Nineteen

The girl was unconscious. Kate ran to her side while the others gathered around. Carl Wilson was already on the phone to 911.

"What happened?" Kate asked Ronda as she opened the girl's eyes to see if her pupils were equal sizes. She seemed to be breathing.

"I don't know," Ronda said. "We were just talking about the *Fashionista* party, and then . . ."

As she spoke, Ashley's eyes fluttered open.

"What happened?" she said.

Kate gazed down at her. Her face was unbelievably pale, yet she smiled at Kate.

"You passed out," Kate said. "There's an ambulance coming."

Ashley sat up then, alarmed. "No," she said. "Don't call an ambulance. I'm fine."

"But, honey, you collapsed," Kate said, trying to calm her.

"I won't go," she reiterated. "I'm fine. I really am. I just need a little food in my stomach, and I'll be good as new."

Kate met Angie's eye, and the girl went to the kitchen to find something for Ashley to eat.

"Call them back," Ashley said, her eyes searching Kate's. "I don't want to worry my folks. Really, I'm fine. Just get me some food, please."

Kate didn't miss her glance at Carl.

Still, Kate wasn't so sure.

Angie returned a few minutes later with crackers and cheese and a glass of juice. Ashley gratefully ate, and her color started to return. Kate heard the sound of sirens outside.

"Please tell them to go away," Ashley begged Kate. "I won't go with them."

"Just let them look at you," Kate said. "If they say you're okay you don't have to go." Finally the girl conceded.

Kate saw the pained look in her eyes as they listened to her heart and took her blood pressure. Finally the Emergency technician turned to Kate and said, "She seems okay. Could've been anything." He turned back to Ashley. "Did you get up too fast?"

She shrugged. "Perhaps." But Kate saw the uncertainty pass in her eyes as if she was afraid of being caught in a lie.

The emergency personnel must not have noticed it, because they had her sign a form and were on their way.

A MESSAGE FROM MOUSE finally came on Friday morning, though it looked as if it had been sent late the previous night.

I told my boyfriend I'm pregnant, and now he hates me. What can I do, Mrs. Hanlon? I knew it would be hard, but not this hard. When we first started going out, my friends warned me not to date a boy who was so much older than I was. I should have known he didn't really love me. People talk about unconditional love, but I don't believe it exists. At least I haven't seen it. I sure didn't see it when I told him the news.

My dad will be even more angry because there's no way the two of us will ever get married. You don't know my dad. He expects his children to be perfect. And the thing is, I'm most sad that I've let him down, and myself. I know you said that my life isn't over, and I really want to believe that, but I'm not seeing it. As far as everything I love, my life is over. I'll never go to college, never make something more of myself.

I don't know about this adoption thing. I think that would be hard too. There is no good answer, at least not anymore. It's too late for good answers.

Thank you for talking to me. I know you're trying to help me even though I can't tell you who I am. I really wanted to tell you who I was today, but I couldn't do it. Thank you for caring for me, even if God and my parents and my boyfriend don't care.

Your friend,
Mouse

Kate stared at the screen as her hope began to fade. Kate would have to be much more direct, she decided. She would just have to come out and ask each of the girls if one of them was Mouse. And yet she couldn't do that. There was a reason Mouse had kept her identity secret. If Kate blurted the question out, it would be a breach of respect, and if that was gone,

what else was there? At least Mouse was still e-mailing her.
That was something. When the time was right, she would
reveal herself. Wouldn't she?

What if she did something rash instead, like running
away? Would Kate be able to live with herself?

One thing was clear. There were no easy answers.

Finally she decided to do the only thing she could do:
write the girl back.

Kate clicked the Reply button and stared at the blank
screen. Then with a prayer for wisdom, she began as simply
as she could.

Dear Mouse,

*There's a verse in Romans 8 that says, "I am con-
vinced that neither death nor life, neither angels nor
demons, neither the present nor the future, nor any
powers, neither height nor depth, nor anything else in
all creation, will be able to separate us from the love of
God that is in Christ Jesus our Lord."*

*In other words: Neither poor choices nor good, nei-
ther acting perfect or sinful, neither unwanted pregnancy or graduating at the top of your class can ever
keep God from loving you the way he already does. He
won't ever stop.*

*I can't imagine how difficult all of this is for you,
and I hope more than anything that you'll tell me who
you are so I can help you. I'll even come with you to tell
your parents if you like. Or if you don't want me to do
that, I won't. But I'm here for you. Okay?*

Kate

CARS WAITED in a line that was at least a block long. It snaked from the library all the way down Main Street to Copper Mill Presbyterian. Several of the boys had brought hoses, and Kate had gathered sponges, rags, and soap into a laundry basket that sat on the library's lawn for any and all to access.

Kate, Paul, and the other volunteers were busily washing Copper Mill's vehicles. Justin Jenner, the younger of the two Jenner boys, and Anne Jackson walked up and down Main Street with signs that read "Afterprom Fund-raiser Car Wash" and "This way to a cleaner car," with an arrow pointing to the parking-lot entrance at the library. There were four stations set up with five to seven people at each. They all took turns hosing and scrubbing, with one rinsing and two buffing.

Kate worked alongside Marlee and Brenna, who were giggling every time they got the hose. Marlee seemed to be doing better, though it had only been two days since her grandmother's funeral. Kate was glad that the girl had made the effort to get out and be with her friends. At least she wasn't in her room, isolated.

Even Kim and Chad Lewis had come out for the event. They were laughing at something one of the teens said as they worked side by side on the far side of the parking lot, scrubbing and polishing cars. Chad had taken off of work to come, and Kate was sure that Kim was thankful for the effort.

As Kate reached for a dry towel from a stack on the pavement, she felt a cold splash of water hit her back. She arched away from it.

"Sorry, Mrs. Hanlon," James Jenner said from the adjoining station. The stocky boy had a huge grin on his face.

Kate stood there for a moment with her mouth open,

catching her breath. Straightening, she turned toward James. She pointed a finger at him and warned, "You'd better watch it, buddy!"

"Uh oh. I'm in trouble," he said, ducking behind the car. James laughed, and for a moment, Kate felt like a sixteen-year-old again.

She glanced over at Ashley Williams, who'd also come out to help. Though she looked better than the previous night, she hadn't joined in the laughter, and she seemed quieter than the other times Kate had seen her. Her eyes met Kate's from the front of the car where she was drying with a big beach towel. She glanced away.

It wasn't until Kate saw Carl's Toyota Corolla pull in for a wash that she realized something more was going on. As soon as Ashley spotted him, she picked up her purse and started to leave.

Kate hurried to follow her. "What's wrong?"

"I'm not feeling well," Ashley said.

"Ashley . . . does this have something to do with Carl?"

Ashley stopped walking and stared at her. "What did he tell you?"

"Nothing," Kate said as her heart picked up its pace.

"Good," Ashley said. Then she turned to go. "I need to get home to my folks."

"Ashley . . . wait." Kate knew she was pushing it.

"Really, Mrs. Hanlon. I have to go."

Chapter Twenty

All the next day, Kate thought about Ashley leaving the car wash and waited for an answer to her FriendsForever message. Mouse remained silent.

Paul had gone on another fishing outing with Danny and Sam, so Kate had the house to herself. She felt a stab of resentment that he hadn't mentioned that their first-date anniversary was coming up, but she quickly reminded herself that she too had forgotten the date when he'd asked about taking off on a fishing trip on the eighteenth.

She logged onto her FriendsForever account and perused Ronda's and Ashley's home pages, looking for any clues, but there was nothing new.

The pain in Ashley's eyes the previous day haunted her.

She opened her in-box and clicked over to Mouse's last e-mail, the one that said her boyfriend had taken the news badly.

Had she finally scared Mouse away for good? The thought made Kate's insides ache. She'd only wanted to help, yet it looked as if she'd messed everything up.

Kate tried to keep busy the rest of the day by calling people from town, asking for volunteers to chaperone at the afterprom party, and checking over the remaining details. The rising cost of the event was shocking. Kate was glad the funds were coming from the citizens of Copper Mill. The members of Faith Briar Church never would have been able to afford the event on their own.

She went over the numbers one last time, then laid her binder in its spot on the counter so she'd know where to find it next time she needed it. Then her thoughts turned again to Mouse. Finally she picked up the phone and called Livvy.

"Yesterday morning I told her I'd help her tell her parents the news, and I haven't heard from her since," Kate said. "I'm worried now that that might not have been the best thing to say. Maybe it'll scare her away. It's hard enough to be a responsible married adult and be pregnant with your first child, but to go through something like this when you're young and alone. She seemed so vulnerable in her messages . . ."

"You can only do what you can do," Livvy said. "And God is watching over her."

"I know. Thanks, Liv. I needed that reminder."

KATE WAS GLAD when Monday rolled around. She had an appointment at nine o'clock to rid herself of her orange hair.

All the heads under the dryers turned to take in Kate's neon style when she entered. Kate felt her face flush with warmth.

"Kate, I can't believe you didn't come back sooner to get your hair fixed," Betty said. "It's been almost a week!"

Betty turned to Alicia, one of the other stylists at the shop. "Didn't Ronda make room in her schedule?"

"I scheduled the appointment for Kate," Alicia said. "But I had no idea . . ." Her gaze lifted to the atrocious hair. "I didn't know it was an emergency. Why didn't you tell me, Kate?"

"It's fine, really," Kate said. "Hair is hardly ever an emergency."

"But you've been going around town looking like that?" Betty was clearly appalled.

"It's really not that big a deal," Kate said.

The lines in Betty's face that had been tight and drawn relaxed, and Betty took in a deep breath.

"How can I make these kids learn?" she said quietly. "The customer comes first. That's what I always tell them; we have to make the customer happy."

Kate smiled and patted her arm.

"I still have to make this up to you," Betty insisted.

"As long as you help chaperone the afterprom party with me, I'm happy," Kate said.

"Done!" Betty said, then she paused to think. "But that's not enough. What do you say I take you on a shopping excursion? We'll go to Chattanooga, hit the vintage stores, look for fancy prom attire to really embarrass those teenagers at the Grand March." She grinned mischievously.

Kate smiled. She liked how Betty thought. She hadn't given what she'd wear to the event any consideration, so she held out her hand and said, "It's a deal! But we'll have to bring Livvy along too."

The two women shook on it.

Soon Betty was caught up in dyeing Kate's hair. She set a timer and placed it on the stand next to Kate.

"When that goes off, you'll be done," Betty assured her.

"Just like a stuffed turkey," Kate said dryly.

Betty turned to the next customer, who was waiting on the front bench, and called the woman over.

Betty and Alicia both seemed unusually rushed for time that morning. Every chair in the place was filled with a customer. The stylists scurried from one to the next. It wasn't like them. Finally the reason dawned on Kate.

"Is Ronda here today?" she asked Betty when it was time to rinse her hair.

Betty shook her head no and leaned Kate back over the sink. The warm water soothed Kate's scalp.

"She's out sick again, even though I told her we had a tight schedule."

"Did she say why?"

Betty shrugged and didn't say anything as she gently lifted Kate upright and wrapped a towel around her head.

"Does she have a boyfriend?" Kate asked. Betty gave her a curious look.

Kate took her seat at the hair-cutting station, and Betty began to comb out her wet locks.

"She talks about a boy from Pine Ridge all the time. I think he's in his last year of college." She paused to take a breath, then changed the subject. "Usually she seems to at least care about the quality of her work, and she's the best back-comber I've ever seen. But if things keep going the way they have been, I don't know how I'll be able to keep her on staff." She glanced at Kate's hair.

Kate pictured Ronda's handiwork: the many elderly women in town with hair teased so high that they could have housed small animals inside.

Betty moved to the other side of Kate and combed through her soggy tresses.

"Ronda usually seems on the ball and is very personable. I'd hate to see you lose her," Kate said.

Betty nodded as she reached for the scissors to begin Kate's trim.

"Do you think she'd mind if I stopped by to check on her?" Kate asked. "I mean if I stopped by to see her at home today?"

"I don't see why not." Betty turned toward Kate and placed her hand on her hips as if waiting for an explanation, but Kate didn't say anything else.

RONDA LIVED WITH HER FOLKS in a small apartment over the *Copper Mill Chronicle*. Kate almost missed the door that led up narrow stairs to the tight second-story landing. Betty had told her that Ronda's place was the first apartment on the left, before the hallway disappeared around the corner.

When Kate arrived, there was a note on the door that said, "Ronda, I stopped by, but you were gone. Call me. Will."

Kate wondered who Will was.

She knocked on the door and waited as the sound of padding feet drew near. Finally the ancient wooden door creaked open.

"Mrs. Hanlon?" Ronda said.

She wore a pink bathrobe, and her hair was a tangle, not from backcombing, but from a day spent in bed. She opened the door wider. Her gaze moved to Kate's revived hair.

"You got your hair fixed," she observed.

"Don't worry about my hair," Kate said. "Betty mentioned

that you weren't feeling well, so I thought I'd stop by. Is there anything I can do for you?"

Ronda stepped back, motioning for Kate to follow her into the small two-bedroom apartment that reminded Kate of Mary Tyler Moore's place on the TV show of the same name. The only difference was that this apartment had bedrooms off the main room. It was a cute apartment, with homemade crafts here and there—needlepoint pillows and ceramic dolls with crocheted dresses in glass-fronted display cases.

Ronda climbed onto the sofa and tugged the blankets up around her as she turned off the TV.

"I don't know what it is," she said. "I start feeling better, and then I go back to the salon, and *wham* I'm under it again. I start feeling nauseous, and my eyes get all scratchy . . ."

Kate studied her. She didn't look well. Dark circles lined her eyes despite the sallow pallor of her skin.

What was it with the girls in this town? Kate thought. *Weren't any of them healthy?*

"I'm sure it's nothing," Ronda said. "Like Betty says, it's all in my head."

"Do you think you'll feel up to going back to work soon?" Kate finally said.

"I hope so. I can't afford to keep missing, with all my cosmetology-school loans still to pay off, and . . . everything else."

"How much work have you missed?"

"Too much. I'm convinced it's the perm solution."

"You mentioned before that you thought you were allergic?"

Ronda nodded. "Betty says that people don't just get allergies when they're older, but I've been looking it up online, and she's wrong. People can develop allergies at any time in their lives, and they can go away just like that too."

"So, what are you going to do?"

"It's kind of hard to be a beautician and be allergic to perm solution. I have no idea what I'll do. I'm worried that Betty is ready to fire me as it is."

"Have you seen a doctor?"

Ronda seemed to consider that for a moment. "No, but I probably should. Thanks, Mrs. Hanlon."

"For what?" Kate said.

"For more than you know."

As Kate left the apartment and made her way to the Bixby house to begin preparing Faith Freezer lunches, she felt a sudden confidence that Ronda couldn't be Mouse. Scratchy eyes weren't a known symptom of pregnancy, and to top it off, Ronda didn't seem to have any aspirations beyond Copper Mill as Mouse did.

That left Ashley. She had all the earmarks, all the symptoms. If only she would open up to Kate in person.

When Kate arrived at the old Bixby house, where volunteers for the Faith Freezer Program prepared meals for the needy and homebound in the area, several cars were already parked in the driveway.

Renee Lambert greeted her as she entered and reached for one of the white aprons that hung from a hook along the sink wall. Kate was thrilled to see that Kim Lewis was already there, peeling potatoes for mashing.

"I'm glad you could make it," Kate said to the kindergarten teacher. "Didn't you have class today?"

"No. The kids had off today. One of the benefits of being an elementary school teacher," Kim said. "Chad had some meetings scheduled at the office, or he'd be here too."

Kate tied on an apron and reached for a peeler. She looked forward to spending time with Kim. She thought about mentioning her thoughts about adoption, but she knew it wasn't the time yet.

Renee prepared pork chops at the other side of the room. Dot Bagley stood at the sink peeling carrots.

"So," Kate said, turning toward Kim, "what did you think of the car wash?"

Kim smiled, her gaze still on the spud in her hand. "We had a lot of fun. I like teenagers. I even thought about teaching at the high-school level, but something about those six-year-olds drew me in." She shook her head.

"You like teenagers?" Renee said, looking up. "They don't have manners like we had in our day. Our parents demanded a lot more of us. Sometimes I worry about this generation and its morals—or lack of them."

"Exactly." Dot cut in from her station at the sink. "It seems that every other year I hear about some teenager who's pregnant or into drugs. It's just a shame what those kids get themselves into." She turned her plump body to the side and caught Kate's gaze.

"Have you heard anything recently?" Kate asked, her heartbeat picking up.

"Well, no, can't say that I have. But it's just a matter of time."

When Kate glanced at Kim, she noticed that she was shaking. Her back was turned to Kate.

"Kim . . . ," Kate said, placing a hand on the young woman's shoulder.

Kim shrank from her touch.

"What's wrong?" Kate whispered.

Kim shook her head, so Kate leaned next to her ear and whispered, "Would you like to talk about it outside?"

The young woman nodded, and they moved onto the front walk of the old house.

"What's going on?" Kate asked.

Kim drew a shuddering breath and wiped a hand across her cheek. Her eyes searched some distant spot before she spoke. "It's just hard to hear about others being pregnant when it's the one thing I want so desperately."

Kim lifted her eyes. The sadness there broke Kate's heart. She embraced Kim in a long hug and the young woman shook with sobs.

"I'm sorry," Kim finally said. "Volunteering was supposed to help me forget about my woes. And here I am bawling my eyes out."

"Don't worry about it," Kate assured her.

Kim shook her head. "I don't know, I guess I've always pictured Chad and me as parents. It's hard to give that up."

"Of course it is."

"Do you think our time will ever come?"

"That's hard to say," Kate said. "But you can't stress over what you can't control."

Kate wished she could tell Kim about Mouse's baby, but Mouse had given no indication that she was ready or willing to talk about adoption, and until that time came, Kate couldn't bring it up.

After Kim calmed down, Kate placed an arm around her shoulders and led her back into the house, where the smells of baking pork chops and thyme filled the air.

She watched Kim as she returned to her work.

Was Kate's hope that Mouse's baby would find a home with the Lewises simply a dream? What if Mouse never agreed to the idea?

Kate shook her head. Even if this couple wasn't meant to adopt the baby, Mouse still needed a friend. That had to be her focus along with helping the Lewises find the plan that God had for them, regardless of what that plan was.

AFTER THEY'D FINISHED making the food, Kate and Kim packed the boxes to deliver. There were ten names on the list for the day. The recipients changed from week to week, although some remained constant, such as Old Man Parsons. Kate noted that Mr. and Mrs. Edward Williams were on the list and decided to deliver their meal last so she could chat with them. Perhaps they could offer some answers about Ashley.

Kate and Kim tucked the meals into two coolers, then carted them out to Kate's black Honda. The other ladies would clean up the kitchen.

They climbed into the car, and Kate handed the list of names to the younger woman.

"You can navigate," she said. "It should be listed in order of where the houses are arranged in town, but let's do the Williamses' last."

Most of the stops were quick and easy, with a knock on the door and a few minutes of chitchat to make sure everyone was doing well.

Finally they came to the tiny one-story house where the Williamses lived. Kate parked the car and looked at the blue bungalow. The house was set back in a large lot, with maple trees lining the drive and gnarled oaks here and there as if planted by squirrels instead of any kind of landscape design. The backyard dropped away toward Copper Mill Creek.

Kate and Kim made their way to the front door. The curtains were closed, and the house appeared empty at first, until Kate heard the sound of shuffling feet and a woman's voice saying, "I'm coming, I'm coming."

The woman opened the door and smiled when she saw Kate. "I'm Doris," she said, holding a hand out to her.

The woman was a tiny thing, barely ninety pounds. She had a short haircut and brown eyes that sparked with mischief and life.

"I'm glad to meet you," Kate said. "I'm Kate Hanlon, and this is Kim Lewis." She handed the woman her meals.

"It's so nice of you to bring our food," Doris went on. "Our Ashley used to come home from work every day to make lunch for us, but that just wasn't fair to her. She has enough to do at that vet clinic without all the hubbub of preparing our meals."

Kate smiled. "You have a dedicated daughter," she said honestly.

"Most people think that she's our granddaughter," Doris began, and Kate saw a gentleman with a walker move up behind her. "Oh, this is Edward, my husband."

She turned toward the man, who dipped his head to Kate and Kim and said, "Hello."

He had a deep voice that carried authority, and despite the constant shaking of his body, he was a noble-looking man.

His eyes held intelligence and kindness, and when he looked at his wife, Kate could see years of devotion in his gaze.

Doris continued, "We were in our late forties when Ashley was born . . . It's a long story."

Kate wondered for a moment if it was a story that might be helpful to Kim, but then she decided to let it go. Kim didn't need any more reminders of her infertility.

"Maybe we could talk sometime," Kate said, hoping Doris would take the bait.

Doris opened the door wider. "Come on in. We'd enjoy the company."

Kate exchanged glances with Kim. "Do you have some-where you need to be?" she asked.

Kim said no, so they went inside. The first thing that struck Kate was the stunning view from the living room. The north side of the house was one long room with divided-pane windows facing the valley. Whoever had designed the place was an expert on lighting, because sunlight flooded the space, making it feel almost like being in the great outdoors. The misty valley and distant hills spread out before them.

The room was decorated with handmade crafts everywhere and porcelain figurines of birds and cats and assorted farm animals placed on shelves throughout the space.

Doris led them to the dining room, where she and Edward had already set the table for lunch.

"It seems rude of us to eat in front of you," she said.

"Oh, we ate at the Bixby House," Kate said. "Don't worry about us." She smiled at Kim, who seemed a bit stiff and unusually quiet.

"We don't have much company these days," Doris said,

handing Edward a napkin. "The Parkinson's has really taken its toll," she added in a low tone meant just for Kate.

They bowed their heads for a quick prayer, then looked up. Edward dug into his pork chop, his hand shaking while Doris sipped her lemonade.

"So, what did you want to talk about?" Doris said.

"I've really enjoyed getting to know Ashley. Does she have many friends her own age?" Kate asked. "I know she's friends with Ronda . . ."

"How do you know Ashley?" Edward asked as if just entering the conversation.

Kate smiled. "I was at the vet clinic with a friend recently, and Ashley and I got to talking. She's helping with the after-prom party I'm organizing for the Copper Mill High School students."

"Yes, she told us about that. That's just like her, isn't it?" Doris turned to her husband.

Edward's eyes twinkled. He winked at Kate. "Doris is a proud mama," he said.

"Do you have any children, Kate?" Doris asked.

"I have three," Kate said. "A son and two daughters."

She glanced at Kim and didn't miss the hint of pain that crossed her eyes.

"So," Kate said, wanting to return the subject to Ashley, "what were you saying about Ashley's friendships?"

"Oh, right. She doesn't have as many friends as when she was in high school. She does have a boyfriend, but he hasn't come around lately. Carl . . . what is his last name?" Doris looked to her husband who gave her a blank look. "He's older than her. Nice young man."

Doris paused to take a bite of her vegetables. "She hasn't said anything about him lately."

"What's their relationship like?" Kate asked.

"Ashley sure is smitten," Doris said. "They better hurry up and get married, or I'll never have grandchildren."

The irony of her words wasn't lost on Kate. She glanced at Edward, who had been quiet through much of the meal. He seemed a no-nonsense sort of man, who spoke only when absolutely necessary, and if he did, those around had better take heed. He raised a fork to his mouth, his hand shaking visibly, and Kate realized that even if he wasn't a judgmental man, any daughter would be crushed if she hurt him.

Chapter Twenty-One

Finally Mouse responded to Kate's message. A letter was waiting in Kate's home mailbox that afternoon when she got home from the Williamses'. It seemed forever since her last message, though in reality it had only been a few days.

Kate studied the Copper Mill postmark and the penmanship that had become so familiar before sliding her finger inside the flap and opening the envelope. It was the same Hello Kitty stationery as the first letter. It read:

Dear Mrs. Hanlon,

I'm writing a letter to you because the computer at my house isn't working right, and I haven't been able to get to the library to write from there. You've probably wondered what happened to me. I know you're trying to reach out to me. A part of me is glad for that, but another part—a very big part—is scared. Adults say things that they don't mean all the time. I'm not trying to accuse you of anything, but I can't have you telling my parents what's going on. I just can't.

Before, the pregnancy didn't seem real. Oh, I knew I was pregnant, but now I'm seeing it for myself. My body is starting to change, and I've been feeling sick. I wake up feeling green. Someone is bound to get suspicious. I snuck a box of saltine crackers into my room so I can eat them before I get up in the morning. Everyone is too busy to notice that anything is different with me, but I know my dad. He sees everything, like a hawk. He watches me. I think he might suspect already.

I have to tell him. I know I do. I don't know what I'm waiting for—maybe a miracle? You're a pastor's wife —could you pray for a miracle for me? I suppose not. If God had wanted me to have a miracle, he would've thought of that before all this happened.

I've been thinking about what you said about adoption. I tried to look online at some adoption agencies before our computer got wonky. I don't know. It's hard to think about having this baby, but then it's hard to think of giving my baby to a total stranger.

So, I guess all of this is to say that I want you to keep writing to me, but please don't ask who I am. Your e-mails are the only thing I have to hold on to right now. I am so alone.

Mouse

Kate closed her eyes and said a prayer right there for the girl. It was so hard to leave her in the hands of God when she wanted to help her. Yet she knew she didn't have a choice.

KATE STOPPED IN at the Mercantile later that afternoon. She had a few groceries to pick up for her and Paul, and she wanted to talk to Sam Gorman. The bell above the door tinkled when she entered the cluttered store. Arlene Jacobs was at the counter checking customers out.

"Is Sam around?" Kate asked her when she'd finished with the customer she was helping.

"He's in the back."

When Kate neared the meat section, she caught sight of him standing in front of the swinging saloon doors that separated the main store from the back stockroom.

The store owner was a stocky man with a permanent tan and a ready smile. He reminded Kate of a sea captain. The lines around his eyes deepened when he smiled.

"Is there something I can help you find, Kate?" Sam asked.

"Actually, Sam," Kate said. "There is something I was wondering if you could help me with." She pulled the second letter from her purse and held it out to Sam. "Do you carry this kind of stationery?" With the first letter, she didn't have reason to think that the stationery itself might be significant, but since both letters bore the same design, Kate figured there might be a bigger theme going on.

Sam glanced at it, nodding almost immediately. Kate tucked it back in her handbag before he could read its intimate contents.

"It's over here." Sam led the way to the aisle that contained school supplies and stationery.

"I hardly pegged you as a Hello Kitty kind of person, Kate," Sam teased as he pointed out the stationery on a shelf near the bottom.

"It's not for me," Kate said, not wanting to go into too much detail. "Have you carried this kind for long?"

"No," Sam said, "I'd say we started carrying it within the last couple of months. Why?"

"No reason," Kate said. "Do you know who might've bought some?"

"Kate, are you sleuthing again?" Sam raised an eyebrow.

Kate smirked. "Maybe . . ."

"The paper's popular with all the young girls. It could've been anyone. Hello Kitty, I would say, is more for the young set."

"Or maybe if it's an older girl it's someone who isn't afraid of being out of sync with her peers . . . ," Kate added, distracted by her churning thoughts.

As SHE MADE HER WAY down Main Street toward the veterinarian clinic to see Ashley, Kate couldn't get her mind off her talk with Sam. Ashley Williams didn't strike Kate as the kind of young woman who wasn't afraid to stand out. She was more a tan-and-khaki kind of girl. Maybe even camouflage.

Yet the clues all added up.

Ashley lifted her eyes from the computer screen when Kate came in. Her brow furrowed, and she said, "Mrs. Hanlon, did you finally get a dog?"

"No," Kate laughed, realizing it probably did seem odd to come to a vet clinic without an animal in tow.

"Your hair is back to normal."

"Yes, it feels good not to look like a carrot."

The dark-haired girl laughed, and Kate smiled, imagining herself with an actual carrot on her head.

"So . . . ," Ashley finally said, "what brings you here?" She raised her eyebrows in question.

"Actually, I dropped by to see you. I saw your folks earlier today."

"Is Dad okay?" Ashley started to rise.

"Oh, they're fine," Kate assured, motioning for her to sit back down. "I was delivering their Faith Freezer meals."

Ashley placed a hand on her chest. "I always worry about Dad," she said, releasing a heavy breath.

"Did you ever tell them that you passed out at the church?" Kate asked.

"Oh . . ." Ashley shrugged. "No, I didn't. I didn't want to worry them. I'm okay now anyway."

"But there had to be a reason for it. People don't just pass out for no reason." Kate knew she was pushing. She hoped it would be the encouragement the girl needed.

"I'm fine now." Her lower lip quivered, and she turned her face away.

"Ashley . . . What's wrong?"

"Like I said, it's nothing. I think you should go."

Chapter Twenty-Two

After getting dinner started Kate decided to make bread pudding for the counseling session with Kim and Chad that night. It was a rich recipe that called for day-old croissants and heavy whipping cream, with raisins scattered throughout.

Its tantalizing scent began to fill the kitchen as Kate plugged in her laptop computer to check her messages on FriendsForever. She waited for the connection, then clicked on the link.

Kate stared at the words on the screen. It had been sent earlier in the day, before she'd gone to see Ashley.

I've been thinking about what to do. Whether I should raise my baby or maybe . . . It's hard to even consider it. But maybe adoption is the way to go. I don't know anything about adoption . . . Do you? I don't know if it's something I'd want to do or not, and yet I wonder if it would be a better choice for my baby.

Tell me about this couple. What are they like? Do you really think they'd be interested in adopting my baby?

Mouse

Kate closed her eyes, praying she hadn't destroyed all she'd worked so hard to build. Then she reread the e-mail.

She knew the words must have been hard for the girl to write, and Kate's heart ached for her. What sort of pain would Kate have suffered if she'd given one of her three children to strangers to raise?

Kim and Chad Lewis' faces came to mind. Kate didn't want to tread where God didn't intend, and yet something inside her told her it was right. The time had come.

Kate did some online research to gather local information on adoption for herself as much as for Mouse and the Lewises, should they be interested. She found a reputable adoption agency's site in Chattanooga. She'd heard of the agency before and knew them to be above board. She clicked on the link that said "Are You Pregnant?" The next page contained information on finding counseling, talking to an adoption attorney, as well as getting prenatal care and additional health insurance.

Kate copied the hyperlink and sent it to Mouse.

WHEN KIM AND CHAD LEWIS came for their counseling session, they seemed to be doing much better. They sat a little closer on the couch and were even holding hands.

"So," Paul clapped his hands and leaned forward in his chair. "How has this week gone?"

Kim smiled. "It's been a good week," she began. "Helping with the car wash and at the Faith Freezer ... You were right about getting the focus off of our problems. It was really good for us, for me."

Chad squeezed her hand, though his smile seemed

somewhat tentative. Kate looked at him and wondered if there was something he wanted to say, but then he turned to study his wife while she spoke.

"My insecurity has been ruining our marriage," Kim confessed. "I surprised Chad with a picnic lunch earlier this week, but when I saw how buried he was in work and how stressed, I realized I was being ridiculous."

"But I *was* avoiding being with her," Chad confessed. "I could've brought work home. At least then I'd have been with her."

"We apologized to each other." Kim glanced from Kate to Paul. "What you said about believing the best about each other really stuck with me. I'd been thinking that Chad hated me and blamed me for not being able to carry a baby to term."

"I guess I was blaming myself," Chad said. "And I was angry with Kim for still holding on to a dream that obviously isn't going to happen."

Even with Chad's continued pessimism toward the couple's fertility, Kate was amazed at the difference a week could make. She sat back in her chair. Chad glanced at Kim. Kate could see the love he had for his wife in his eyes.

"This is progress," Paul said, a smile on his face. "I'm very encouraged, for both of you."

Husband and wife both nodded their agreement.

"I'm glad to see that you've stopped playing the blame game," Paul went on. "Forgiveness is what makes a marriage work."

Kate gazed at Kim and Chad, thinking of how desperately they wanted a child. It had been so easy for her and Paul to have children. When they decided to have kids, the kids just came.

"Kate and I have been talking about your situation," Paul said, pulling Kate's attention back into the conversation. "We were wondering if you've ever thought about adoption."

Kate was surprised that he'd brought it up since he'd said he didn't think the Lewises were ready yet. The expression on Kim's face said they'd had this discussion many times. She glanced at Chad, who seemed to stiffen at the comment. He took a quick sip of his water.

"We have talked about it," Chad began. "There are risks with adoption too. I don't think we could survive it if a birth mother decided to take her baby back after we'd had it. I know Kim thinks she can handle it, but I'm not so sure she can . . ." His words faded.

"I'm willing to take the chance," Kim said. Then she seemed to think again and shook her head. "But maybe Chad is right. When I miscarried, I became so depressed . . ."

"I have a friend," Kate said. Chad and Kim turned to look at her. "Maybe you know her. Betty Anderson?"

Kim nodded, though only slightly, so Kate wasn't sure if that meant she knew Betty or was just listening intently.

"I wonder if talking to her and her husband would help." Kate glanced at Paul. "She and Bob have gone through a lot of the same things you have, with infertility and miscarriage. I think she might be able to offer some comfort and insight."

"Did they adopt their children?" Chad asked.

"Yes," Kate said. "Their first son, anyway. Their second son is biological. But I think because they've been in your shoes, they might be able to help you work through some of the issues that Paul and I aren't as familiar with. I haven't talked to them about it, so I'd have to see if they were willing . . ."

Kate saw the expression of hope in Kim's eyes and the doubt in Chad's. If only he could see how wonderful adoption could be, as Kate had seen it in Betty's eyes the day they'd talked about it at the salon.

"We can talk to her," Chad finally said. Kim squeezed his hand, and he smiled. "What can it hurt, right? But I'm a private person. I don't necessarily want to lay out my life story for a stranger."

"Of course," Kate agreed. "You don't have to share anything you're uncomfortable sharing. I'll give Betty a call tonight."

"WE'D BE HAPPY TO TALK TO THEM," Betty said when Kate called right after the Lewises left. "It's hard to comprehend the feeling of loss that comes with not being able to have your own kids unless you've been there. It's as if you've had your mind made up your whole life about how things are supposed to work, and when they don't . . . it's like the death of something."

Kate was glad she'd thought to ask Betty and Bob Anderson if they could talk to Kim and Chad. The Lewises were bound to be encouraged by her story, to know that another couple had gone through what they were going through and had come out on the other side with a happy and vibrant marriage.

KATE LIFTED HER FACE to the ceiling as she sat on the bed in their bedroom that night. She couldn't stop thinking about Ashley. Was she Mouse?

"Lord, help me find this girl. And help her to have the courage to tell me who she is."

Mouse had seemed desperate for a friend, yet when Kate had tried to reach out to Ashley, she'd resisted. Maybe she was Mouse, too afraid of telling her parents to take that risk. Or maybe Kate had been on the wrong track all along.

Just then, Paul came in from the living room.

"What's wrong?" he asked.

Kate shook her head. "I felt I was getting close to discovering who Mouse was, but I'm not so sure anymore."

"Meaning?" He tilted his head.

"If it's Ashley, why won't she open up to me? How am I going to help her if I can't break through?"

"You have been helping her," Paul reminded. "On FriendsForever."

Kate knew Paul was right. It took some getting used to, thinking of a Web site as her portal to helping a living, breathing person, but this was where the girl came to find support and hope.

WHILE PAUL WAS GETTING READY for bed, Kate padded into the study and booted up the computer. She waited several long minutes to connect to the Internet, then she clicked open her FriendsForever page and went to her in-box. Her heart skipped when she saw another message from Mouse.

Dear Mrs. Hanlon,

Thanks for the link to the adoption agency. I'll look into it later when I know no one will be looking over my shoulder.

You have become my only friend these days.

Don't worry that I haven't told my folks yet. But I can't keep it secret much longer. The way Dad's been treating me lately, it's as if he already knows. I tried to tell him today. I'd only told him that me and my boyfriend broke up, and he went off on me about how he didn't like him in the first place, and that's what I get for going out with someone so much older than me. He'll freak when I tell him the rest.

I've been thinking that it'd be easier to just run away, but I can't do that to my mom. I want to tell you who I am. I really do.

But I just can't. Can you understand that?

Mouse

Kate wanted to shout at the computer that she couldn't understand it. She couldn't understand it at all.

Chapter Twenty-Three

When Kate got home from running errands the next morning, there was a message on her answering machine. The little red light was blinking off and on. She punched the Play button, and Livvy's voice came on.

"Kate, it's Livvy. There was an ambulance at the vet clinic about half an hour ago. I heard that they took Ashley Williams to the ER. I thought you might want to know."

Kate immediately thought of Ashley's parents and wondered if they knew and were able to come to the hospital. Pulling out the Copper Mill phone book, she found their number and dialed, but there was no answer. Kate assumed that meant they were at the hospital with Ashley already. She quickly wrote a note for Paul and then ran back to the car.

A thousand thoughts battered her mind as she drove the torturous miles to the hospital in Pine Ridge. The drive felt eerily familiar as she recalled trying to find Mouse the time before. What if Ashley really was Mouse? Would she lose the baby this time? What exactly had happened?

The medical center was a one-story brick building in the heart of Pine Ridge. Kate parked and got out of her car, climbing the steps to the ER door. The receptionist raised her head.

"I'm looking for Ashley Williams," Kate said.

She pointed Kate to the waiting room where she spotted Doris and Edward Williams. The petite elderly woman paced the small waiting room, wringing her delicate hands. Edward was sitting. His head was bent down as if in prayer, and Kate saw the tremor in his shoulders.

Kate immediately went over to Doris. "I heard about Ashley and wanted to see if there was anything I could do," she said.

Doris grasped her hand for a moment and then patted it before letting go.

"Have you heard anything?" Kate asked.

"She passed out at work," Edward said. "When they couldn't revive her, they called the ambulance."

Kate sat with them for what seemed an eternity before the lanky dark-haired doctor appeared with news.

"She's awake," Dr. McLaughlin said. Doris sighed in relief.

"Why did she pass out?" Edward asked, rising to stand beside his wife. His legs shook, and he held onto a chair.

"She's hypoglycemic . . . Has she been diagnosed before?" the doctor asked.

Finally it all came to Kate—the weight gain, the nausea, the sudden fainting episodes. It all added up.

"Her glucose levels were so low, it's a miracle she's even here," the doctor said, drawing Kate's attention back to the conversation. "We're going to need to keep her for a day to get her blood sugar regulated and get her on a healthy diet."

Edward and Doris nodded. Kate placed a comforting hand on Doris' back. The woman glanced at her with a tear-filled smile.

"So her weight gain and nausea were symptoms of hypoglycemia?" Doris asked the doctor.

Dr. McLaughlin nodded.

"I knew something was wrong," she said, looking to Edward. "She'd break out in a cold sweat and get so jittery, but she hates to be dependent on us. She's so independent."

"She's at risk for developing diabetes, and we need to check to make sure the hypoglycemia isn't being prompted by a tumor."

Doris fluttered a hand to her chest, and Edward wrapped his arms around her shoulders.

When she had calmed herself, she asked, "Can we go see her?"

"Of course," the doctor said. "I'll get a nurse to show you where she is."

While they waited for the nurse, Doris said, "Would you like to come see Ashley too?"

"This is your time with your daughter. I wouldn't want to intrude."

"I'd feel better if you came," the sweet woman insisted.

Kate finally conceded and followed with Doris and Edward as the nurse led the way to Ashley's room a few minutes later. She was hooked up to a heart monitor and had an IV in her arm. Her skin was just getting its color back.

She turned her head toward them and smiled. "Sorry about all this," she said in a weak voice.

"Oh, Ashley." Her mother moved next to her bed with her father close behind. He took the chair that flanked the bed, Kate suspected because he had difficulty standing for long.

"Mrs. Hanlon," Ashley said, "it was so nice of you to come."

"I thought your folks could use a little moral support, and I was worried about you." Kate smiled into her eyes, then turned to Doris. "Did someone bring you? Do you have a way home?"

"We have our car," she said, glancing at her husband, who had taken Ashley's hand in his big paw. He had the callused hands of a man used to hard labor. They reminded Kate of her own father's hands.

"I'll be back home in no time," Ashley assured them. "You two need to get some rest. You look tired."

Edward laughed. "We were worried."

"I mean it." Ashley looked at Kate. "Can you make sure they get home and take care of themselves?"

Kate was impressed by the young woman's selflessness.

She touched her warm hand and said, "I'll take care of them if you take care of yourself. Deal?"

Ashley nodded. "Deal."

KATE FOLLOWED DORIS and Edward's car back to Copper Mill. After they had pulled into the driveway, Kate walked them up to the quaint house. Edward offered his thanks, then went inside while Doris lingered with Kate.

"No wonder Ashley's been feeling bad," Kate said.

"She keeps so much to herself. I worry about her." Doris shook her gray head. "We found out that Carl Wilson broke up with her too. She hadn't told us. The poor dear."

Kate squeezed the woman's hand. "She's going to be okay."

"I hope so."

KATE HAD BEEN on the wrong trail all along. When Kate got home, she pulled out the two handwritten messages she'd gotten from Mouse and looked at them. Who was she? And why hadn't Kate been able to find her?

That question was the most troubling of all. Kate had spoken with the girl—she'd said so herself—and yet Kate hadn't been able to guess her identity. Kate was usually so good at intuiting such things.

She turned to lay her handbag on the kitchen table when she saw a package on the counter alongside the day's mail. Paul must have left it there.

There was no return address, but she knew instantly who it was from. If the loopy handwriting hadn't given it away, the Celtic cross drawn in the bottom left-hand corner would have.

She carefully pulled the red string across the top to open it. Inside was a beautiful scarf. It looked handmade with fine embroidered flowers running its length, and a tiny mouse peeking its head out of the foliage. On one end were Kate's initials in a delicate font. The note inside read:

Dear Mrs. Hanlon,

I made this especially for you. I hope you like it. I feel like I have a friend in you, and that is something new for me. Thanks.

Mouse

Staring at the beautiful scarf, Kate couldn't help but think that it was an important clue. Suddenly, a fog started to lift.

KIM AND CHAD ARRIVED early for their meeting with Betty and Bob Anderson on Thursday. Kate had made a batch of oatmeal cookies and a fresh pot of coffee, which she set on the coffee table alongside the cups and napkins and cream and sugar.

Chad was on the edge of his seat again, as he seemed to be whenever he was nervous. Or maybe he was ready to flee, Kate thought. It was practically the starting pose for a three-hundred-meter dash. Kim touched his arm in a comforting way, and she leaned toward his ear to whisper something to him.

Kate had seen a real change in the way this couple related to each other. It seemed they'd taken her and Paul's advice to heart, which was deeply gratifying and humbling at the same time.

Finally the doorbell rang, and Paul went to answer it. Betty was there with a huge grin on her face. She stepped inside, followed by her husband, Bob. He was a smallish man, but he had an easy way about him that complemented Betty's sometimes flamboyant side. They followed Paul to the living room, where he made introductions. Chad and Kim stood to shake their hands, and Kate came over motioning to the coffee and cookies she'd set on the coffee table earlier.

Once everyone was settled, Paul turned to Betty and Bob. "Thanks for coming. We've been counseling Chad and Kim for a little while," he began. "We thought your experiences would help them." He nodded to the couple.

"And," Kim took over, "we want to thank you for being willing to meet with us." She blew out a breath that spoke of the raw emotion that was churning inside her.

Betty, who was in the chair closest to the couch where Kim and Chad were, reached out to touch the pretty kindergarten teacher on the sleeve. "Oh, honey. I know how hard this is. Believe me. We've been there. Do you have specific questions, or would you like us to start with our story? I'm sure it's not too far off from what you're facing. These stories never are, you know."

Kate motioned for her to go on, and Kim nodded as if getting a word out was too much for her. Then she reached for her husband's hand as Betty began to talk.

"We'd always wanted babies," Betty said. "Not like some people who are gaga over little ones, but it'd always been a part of our plan from the time we first talked about getting married. Well, you know how it goes. You're married a while, then you think you're ready. And nothing. Then you finally get the news you want . . . You're pregnant and so excited."

Betty inhaled as if the memory were fresh and not of something that had happened twenty-some years before. "We

thought we were like everyone else. Then we lost that child."
She patted Bob's hand, and his eyes crinkled into a smile as
he gazed at her. "Then we lost the next and the next. It was
devastating. Each time, my hopes soared so high, only to be
crushed. The doctors were no help at all, even though they
charged us an arm and a leg to try to find answers. But there
were no easy solutions."

Kate turned her head to watch Kim and Chad. The mois-
ture in Kim's eyes said she understood Betty's story all too
well. Chad placed his free hand on top of hers, then he
stroked his wife's arm.

"It was as if a part of me died each time," Betty went on.
"And then to come to the realization that we might never
have children. I tell you, I grieved over that for many months.
Wouldn't talk about it, not even with Bob."

Kate saw the expression of guilt cross Chad's face as he
glanced at Kim. But Kim was watching Betty, dabbing at her
eyes with a tissue.

"We had a friend who told us that there were children
who needed families just as much as we needed a child."
Betty smiled. "It's just like getting married. People can tell
you all about it, and you can understand it in your head, but
until you look it square in the face and decide 'I can do this'
it isn't real to you. But then when you see those children, as
perfect as any other child . . ." Her voice trailed off, and she
touched a hand to her collarbone. "You understand that one
of these precious babies might be the one God has planned
for you."

She sat upright and went on. "We adopted George, our
eldest. He was—and still is—the light of our life. He's

thoughtful and talented, just an amazing kid. Then miracle of miracles, I got pregnant again and carried to term. I don't know if it was that I was so much more relaxed or what, but I didn't even have preterm labor with John. So there we were. George was ten months old, and he already had a little brother. That only happens in adoption, I tell you."

She laughed. Kate glanced at Kim, who seemed mesmerized by the story. The tears on her cheeks had dried, replaced by a growing smile.

The same could not be said of her husband.

Chad leaned his forearms on his thighs. His lips were pursed in thought, his expression troubled.

"Chad?" Paul beat Kate to the punch. "Was there something you wanted to ask?"

"Yeah," the young accountant said. "I don't know how this will sound . . ."

"Feel free to express your honest feelings," Kate said.

"And not everyone is meant to adopt," Betty added.

Chad nodded, then finally found the courage to say, "Not all adoptions end so well . . ."

He paused, and a troubled expression passed over his face. "Some children really struggle with the whole idea of not knowing who they are. Some birth mothers decide to take their babies back. Adoption isn't always a bed of roses."

"That's true," Betty said. "Sometimes those things do happen. Sometimes bad things happen to families with biological children too. I think my John struggled more with identity issues than George ever did."

"What if I don't . . . bond with a child? Does everyone just automatically love their adopted child?"

Paul said, "Bob, do you want to answer?"

Bob dipped his bald head and pursed his lips in thought, then he said, "Let me say that even biological parents don't automatically feel love for or attachment to their children. Sometimes it grows with time, just like falling in love with your spouse. But once you invest yourself and start to take care of that little person, the feelings just come."

Chad seemed to think on that for a while. Kate wished she knew what was going on inside Chad's head.

AFTER THE LEWISES and the Andersons had gone, Kate and Paul sat together at the kitchen table. Their coffee had grown cold.

"What do you think?" Kate asked.

Paul shook his head. "It's hard to say. Chad seemed . . . closed."

"It seems like Kim's on board. I fear it'll break her heart if Chad can't agree."

"I know." He met Kate's eyes. "All we can do at this point is pray." He grasped her hand in his, and they bowed their heads.

"Lord," he began, "we want your will for the Lewises, and we know how you feel about adoption. You've adopted us as your children. But whatever plan you have for them, please work it out for their good and also for the good of this unborn baby. Please relieve Chad of whatever is holding him back, whether or not it leads to adoption. Because we know that fear is never part of your plan. We ask you to keep their marriage strong. Teach them to rely on each other, to be each other's best friend. Like you've made Katie and me."

Kate glanced at Paul and realized she still felt a stab of disappointment that he'd seemingly forgotten the anniversary of their first date. It surprised her because she'd thought the matter was settled in her heart. Paul lifted his gaze and smiled at her.

Then she realized that she knew Paul better than that. He loved her, and even if he had forgotten one small anniversary, she didn't have the right to hold it over his head.

Chapter Twenty-Four

The finale party for *Fashionista* was Friday, as was Paul's overnight fishing trip with Sam and Danny. Danny's boys, James and Justin, had talked their dad into letting them come along too, so Kate invited Livvy to join the girls for the sleepover.

Several girls had e-mailed that they would be able to come, including Ronda, who agreed to show the girls how to do their hair, as well as Ashley, who insisted she was as good as new despite her hospital stay earlier in the week. Brenna Phillips, Marlee Jones, Anne Jackson, and Angie Petzel had also accepted Kate's invitation.

After the events of the week, including Ashley's hospital trip and the package that arrived from Mouse, Kate felt more confident than ever that she finally knew who the girl was. And hopefully the sleepover would allow Kate to get her alone so she could once and for all know the truth.

THE *FASHIONISTA* MODELS moved along the runway like cats slinking, each stopping at the end to strike a pose and set their faces in stonelike expressions. Not one of them wore a smile. Kate was amused at the spectacle, while the girls seemed mesmerized, especially Angie. Anne Jackson had yet to arrive.

The three designers stood at the ready—one in Jackie-O perfection, another in a 1980s Madonna-Michael Jackson-type getup, and the third in a basic pencil skirt and silk blouse.

"And the winner of the $100,000 prize and a chance to study with famed designer Libertine . . . ," the announcer of the show said as a drum rolled for a bated-breath moment. "Mariana Sciana from Philadelphia."

The woman in the pencil skirt threw her hands to her face in surprise as the other two gathered around.

The girls applauded wildly as the announcer interviewed the winner. When the credits finally rolled, Kate turned off the television.

"I can't believe she won," Marlee said, excitement glowing in her eyes.

She seemed her old self again even though there were moments throughout the evening when Kate had seen the subdued reminders of fresh grief cloud her eyes. At least she was smiling.

Ashley looked much better too. The color had returned to her cheeks, and she had a healthy glow. She and Ronda sat next to each other on the love seat, as if being each other's moral support with the younger girls around.

Kate glanced at Livvy, who was wearing her pj's and furry zebra-print slippers.

"Did you enjoy it, Liv?" Kate asked.

The librarian shook her head. "I don't get it," she said. "What's the big deal about clothes?"

Brenna tossed a pillow at her, and they all burst out laughing. Kate was glad she'd invited her friend. Livvy seemed to enjoy being around the girls. No doubt living with a houseful of men had something to do with it.

"I like Mariana," Ashley said.

The veterinarian's receptionist often wore the same kinds of outfits at the office, so it was no wonder she preferred the conservative no-nonsense designer.

"Who were you rooting for?" Livvy asked Angie, who blushed.

She shrugged her shoulders. "Oh, I suppose B.J.," she said of the woman in the 1980s outfit. "She wasn't afraid to take chances."

Kate glanced at the piercing in Angie's nose and thought much the same thing about her. She'd been watching Angie throughout the night. The clothes she wore were looser fitting than in the past, and she'd gone to the bathroom on several occasions. She was still thin, but Kate had only known her less than three weeks, so she could have gained a few pounds.

Kate had purposely worn the scarf she'd received in the mail, hoping to get a reaction. Several of the girls had commented on it, but not Angie.

The doorbell rang, and Kate went to answer it. When she reached the door, she discovered a teary-looking Anne.

"Sorry I'm late, Mrs. Hanlon," the pretty girl said.

"Anne, what's wrong?" Kate motioned for her to come inside. She helped the girl with her overnight and sleeping bags and led the way back to the others.

"James broke up with me," she sobbed. "With a text message." Then she caught sight of Livvy and stiffened.

"You poor thing," Livvy said. "He didn't say a word to me. Are you okay?"

The girl seemed to relax then and gave a shrug.

Kate pulled her into a hug, and Livvy came over to talk to her. They moved into Paul's study so they could speak in private. Livvy mouthed to Kate that they would be okay, then she closed the door behind her.

Wasn't spring supposed to be the season of youthful love? Why then did it seem that every young couple Kate knew was breaking up?

"That's rough," Marlee said as Kate returned to the group. "She and James seemed like a really nice couple."

"It happens," Angie said under her breath.

Kate looked at her and studied her serious expression.

Ronda added, "She'll get over him soon enough. We always do."

"So, Mrs. Hanlon," Brenna said, "who did you want to win the show?"

"I haven't been watching the series, so I didn't really have a favorite. Though I liked . . . what was the name of the girl in the pink wool suit?"

The girls answered in unison. "Janine Delilah."

"Her clothes reminded me of when I was young and dating Pastor Hanlon."

"Tell us about it," Ashley said, pulling a pillow onto her lap and sitting up on her sleeping bag, which was rolled out on the living-room floor alongside the other girls' bags.

"Oh, come on. You don't want to hear about a couple of old fogies," Kate said.

"We do too!" the girls protested.

It was clear they weren't about to let Kate off that easily.

Angie leaned in to listen. Kate caught her gaze, and the girl's eyes flitted to the ground.

Kate thought for a moment, then said, "Oh, all right. But don't complain when you discover how boring we are."

The girls groaned and sat up, ready to hear her tale.

"You know that Pastor Hanlon is a few years older than me," she began. "I never thought I'd have a chance with him because he was this handsome bachelor pastor."

"Handsome?" Brenna said, twisting her face into a disgusted expression.

Kate smiled. "You've never noticed his blue eyes?" She placed a dramatic hand on her chest. "They drew me to him like a magnet. Well . . ."—she glanced around at their watchful faces—"a friend of his had this motorcycle. He told Paul he could take it out for a spin after church. He was wearing this black leather jacket. I happened to be just leaving—"

"He took you on a motorcycle ride for your first date?" Marlee said, her voice rising in stunned surprise.

Kate nodded. "I thought we were just going for a spin around the block, but he whispered something to his friend and then took me to a restaurant and a movie. You should've seen my hair after half an hour on a motorcycle—it was a rat's nest! But I didn't care. I was with him. Never in my life would I have thought I'd have that chance. But Paul had planned it out all along. I was too naive to figure it out."

"That is so sweet," Brenna said.

Kate nodded. "Almost thirty years and three children later, we're still here." She shrugged, picturing Paul off on his fishing excursion with the Jenners and Sam.

ONCE LIVVY AND ANNE emerged from the study, the girl seemed to be feeling better, though her eyes still bore the signs of a good cry. Kate pulled out some board games to play, all of which required writing. Kate knew that if she could see the girls' handwriting, she could compare it to the Hello Kitty letters. She wanted to be completely sure before she made any attempts to confront the girl.

"Ooh, Boggle," Ashley said from the other side of the kitchen table, where she was looking through the games with Ronda. "I love Boggle."

Boggle was a word game where the participants searched crossword tiles to see who could find the most and the longest words within the three-minute timespan.

"Who wants to play?" Ashley looked from face to face.

"I'm in," Kate said, then all the girls chimed their approval. "Let's all do a few rounds."

She passed out paper and pens while everyone gathered to sit around the table. Livvy shook the plastic box that held the tiles. When the cubes settled into their slots, she set the box down, and everyone got their pens ready. Kate turned on the three-minute timer, and they all wrote frantically, searching the letters for hidden words. Kate glanced at each of the girls around the table.

At one point or another, she'd been all but positive with several of them that they were Mouse. But when she saw Angie Petzel's handwriting, with its loopy script, she knew.

Angie was Mouse!

Chapter Twenty-Five

Kate wasn't sure how to approach Angie. She certainly didn't want to do it in front of all the others. So she waited, watching Angie and praying for the opportune moment when the two could steal away.

After the group had finished playing Boggle, Ronda demonstrated the proper way to do an updo on Ashley. She tugged and twisted on Ashley's dark hair, adding hairspray and bobby pins until it was a molded coif of curls atop her head. The girls clapped in awe when Ronda finally finished.

When it came time for the group's own little fashion show, there was no contest. Each of the girls came out of Kate's bedroom in the outfit of her choosing, modeling for the rest and turning to strike a pose where the entryway met the living room.

Most wore store-bought outfits with cute tanks peeking out at the neckline and trim-fitting bodices. Angie modeled hers last, a stunning knee-length dress with gold beading along the neckline.

"Where did you get that?" Marlee asked, reaching to touch the fabric from her spot on one of the overstuffed chairs.

Angie shrugged and said in a small voice, "I made it."

"From a pattern?" Brenna Phillips asked, still wearing an orange outfit that reminded Kate of a mechanic's jumpsuit.

"No, I designed it."

Mouths dropped open, and Kate stood up.

"She wins all the prizes," Ronda said with a smile on her face.

Everyone laughed, and Angie blushed.

Kate went into her stained-glass studio to retrieve the prizes she'd made especially for the event.

"I don't know about all of you," she said, standing along-side Angie, "but I'm very impressed with everyone's efforts. So, the prize for the most wearable"—she turned to Ashley—"goes to Ashley Williams for the beautiful shawl she knit."

Ashley's face turned red, though she was grinning from ear to ear. Kate handed her a small sun catcher she'd made in the shape of a dragonfly. After Ashley oohed and aahed over it for a few minutes, Kate handed Anne Jackson the prize for the trendiest outfit. She'd modeled a colorful multilayered outfit. That prize was another sun catcher, a bit bigger than the first, of a sunflower surrounded by blue sky.

"And finally for the most creative outfit: Angie," Kate said, lifting the grand prize for all to see. It was a Celtic cross in shades of gray and blue. The design had been intricate, the cutwork meticulous, but it had turned out perfectly.

Kate looked at Angie as she spoke. The eighteen-year-old's eyes brimmed with tears. She took the cross in her hands and lightly touched its surface.

"It's stunning," she breathed. She lifted her eyes to Kate's. "I adore Celtic crosses."

"I know you do," Kate said, offering a smile of understanding.

IT HAD BEEN THE WRONG PLACE to show Angie that she knew. She could see that the moment the words came out of her mouth. Angie's eyes widened, and she swallowed hard. Thankfully none of the other girls seemed to catch on that something else was going on. They chatted to one another about the contest and played with each other's hair long into the night.

As soon as the teens seemed distracted enough, Kate told Livvy she was going to talk to Angie.

"I'll be praying," Livvy whispered.

Then Kate motioned to the girl, and they slipped into Paul's office, shutting the door behind them for privacy.

"How did you know?" Angie said, her voice cracking with sudden emotion.

"Angie, you wouldn't have kept contacting me if you didn't want me to figure it out. As long as your identity was secret, there was only so much support I could offer you. I'm here for you."

Angie lowered her head. Kate waited for her, patiently, until she finally lifted her face.

"I've been so alone," she said.

Kate reached for her hand.

"And so stupid."

"You're not stupid," Kate said. "Does anyone else know about the baby?"

Angie shook her head. "Just my boyfriend . . . ex-boyfriend I mean. I don't know how many people he's told. He said that he loved me. That lie hurt almost as much as being pregnant."

"How far along are you?"

"Almost three months. I don't know if I'll be able to fit into my prom dress." She shook her head. "I've been sick and still trying to act normal."

"Have you been to the doctor for any physicals since your scare?"

"No. My mom looks those bills over pretty carefully. I managed to grab the insurance claim for the first visit, but the other one . . . I'll have to tell them before that bill arrives." She blew out a heavy breath. "How am I going to tell them?" Angie managed to get out.

Kate remembered how emotional she was with each of her pregnancies, and she hadn't had near the stress that Angie was experiencing.

"I'll help you tell them," Kate assured her. "But you need to tell them soon. You need prenatal care."

"I haven't done anything about contacting that adoption agency you sent me, if that's even the right choice for me. I have no idea what I'm doing," Angie said. "I've been accepted at Parsons New School for Design in New York City next spring. I even have a scholarship. I can't tote a baby along! My mom has enough on her hands with my little sisters. I don't know if she'd be willing to raise my baby, or if that's even a fair question for me to ask her." Her voice rose, and she took a stuttering breath.

Angie closed her eyes and sat back down.

"Let's manage one day at a time, okay?" Kate suggested. "First, we'll tell your folks."

Angie chewed her lower lip. They sat in the quiet for a while, then the teen lifted her face to the simple cross on the wall near the door of Paul's office. "Do you really think God can forgive me?"

"I know so. Angie, your sins are no greater than anyone else's. It's the reason Jesus came. He's in the business of taking awful situations and turning them around. That's what redemption means. He brings beauty from ashes."

"I feel so horrible."

"You're going to have to forgive yourself too."

Angie met her eyes. She swiped the tears from her cheeks, then she smiled. "That's not going to be so easy."

"If God can do it, so can you."

"I only hope my father can do the same."

AFTER THE GIRLS LEFT the next morning, Kate tidied up around the house. She and Angie had decided to break the news to her folks after church the next day. It wouldn't be easy, but then, many necessary things weren't.

A little after four o'clock, Paul arrived home. Kate heard his pickup pull into the driveway. He stomped in the front door and shucked his coat and fishing cap, hanging them on the coat tree that resided there.

Kate rose to greet him, but when she drew near, the smell of lake water and fish was overwhelming. She waved her hand in front of her nose. "What did you do, fall in?"

Paul grinned and kissed her on the nose.

Kate placed her hands on her hips. "Did you have fun?" she asked, teasing.

"We had a great time. You should join us next time."

"I don't think so!" She laughed.

"You should've seen Sam reel in this bass. He was sure it was a monster, the way it fought, but it was a tiny fish. I thought I'd fall out of the boat, I was laughing so hard."

Kate smiled at him, truly glad he'd enjoyed his outing. And even more glad that he was home.

"How was your girls' party?" he asked.

"Good," Kate said. "I found out who Mouse is."

"Who?"

"Angie Petzel."

Paul paused as if trying to remember the girl. "The one with the nose piercing?"

Kate nodded.

He bent over to dig in the Styrofoam cooler he'd brought in with him. Standing, he offered a newspaper-wrapped gift to her. "I almost forgot. I got this for you. I'm sorry it's a day late."

Kate stared at it, stunned. Here she'd thought he'd completely forgotten. She pulled him into a quick hug and then started to open it.

"You might want to open it over the kitchen sink."

Kate gave him a puzzled look. From the feel of it, Kate had a pretty good idea what it was—a nasty, smelly fish. But the expression on Paul's face urged her to go along with him.

So she took the oblong gift into the kitchen and carefully unwrapped it as Paul looked on. Sure enough it was a fish. She lifted questioning eyes to his.

"A fish?" she said, not sure how to react.

"For supper." The grin on his face said there was more.

"Okay, out with it. What's the deal with the fish?"

"Look inside it." His grin went lopsided with mischief.

Kate's stomach turned at the thought of looking into a stinky, slimy fish. She almost walked away, but curiosity held her. Finally, after taking off her wedding and engagement rings and setting them on the counter, she looked in the ribcage that had been cleaned out. Inside was another newspaper-wrapped item, though this one was much smaller. Kate pulled it out and raised an eyebrow at Paul. Kate slowly opened the package to reveal a dinner fork.

"A fork?" Kate said, not sure what to think.

"It comes with a supper at Le Peau's in Pine Ridge and a bed-and-breakfast stay at the Stone Fort Inn in Chattanooga."

Kate gasped, her eyes meeting Paul's. Both places were renowned in the area.

Kate threw her arms around him, smelly or not.

"I thought you forgot," she squeaked as tears came to her eyes.

"I could never forget the time I first fell in love," he said.

"I love you, Paul Hanlon," Kate said.

She kissed him. It was a kiss reminiscent of those they'd shared when their love was new.

KATE REQUESTED THAT ANGIE come by the house so they could chat before going together to tell her parents the news.

The teen arrived at the Hanlons' at one o'clock as Kate was still washing dishes from Sunday lunch.

"Sorry I couldn't get here sooner," she said, pulling out a chair at the oak table.

"You can help me do dishes," Kate said. "Paul was too tired from preaching today, or it'd be his job." She held out a towel for Angie. The girl laughed and joined her at the sink.

"So, why me and Paul?" Kate asked as she dipped a plate into the warm rinse water.

Angie shrugged. "Marlee and Anne told me about you. They said you were . . . cool."

The description made Kate smile. If only her three grown children had been there to hear it.

"They said you're always kind," Angie went on, "and you aren't afraid to get involved in people's lives. I've seen some of the newspaper stories about how you help people." She paused, then said, "I guess I thought if you were willing to help them, you might be willing to pray for me. There isn't anyone at my church that I trust enough to tell. I haven't exactly been the perfect Christian, and I felt that if someone like you was praying for me, God would be more likely to listen."

Kate lifted the pot she'd been scrubbing and dipped it into the rinse water, letting it sink below the surface. Angie pulled it out and let it drip before starting to dry it with the towel.

"Is that what you think? That Christians are perfect?"

Angie shrugged. "Aren't they?"

Kate shook her head. "There's a big difference between perfect and forgiven."

Angie thought about that for a moment. "I guess I can see that."

"When you told your boyfriend"—Kate changed the subject—"what exactly did he say? Is there any chance he'd want to father the baby?"

Angie shook her head sadly. "He doesn't want anything to do with the baby or with me. I told him that I didn't want to marry him. I want to go to Parsons—I've always wanted to go there. Then he had the audacity to suggest that maybe he wasn't even the father . . . I cared about him, you know?" She lifted the next pot out of the sink and dried it. "Last I heard, he was already dating someone else."

Silence lingered between them. Kate placed the last washed dish in the rinse water and let the suds drain out of the sink.

"Have you given any more thought to adoption?" she ventured as she wiped the sink.

Angie nodded, though her eyes showed reservation. "I have. And I think in many ways it could be the right way to go. But until I talk to my folks, I can't really say for sure."

"Of course," Kate agreed.

By two o'clock, everything was back in its rightful spot. Paul had woken up from his nap and meandered out to where Kate and Angie were.

"Are you ready for this?" Kate said as she placed an arm across the girl's thin shoulders.

"Not really."

"Do you want me to come with you?" Paul asked.

Angie shook her head. "No, thank you. My folks probably won't even like having Mrs. Hanlon there. I don't want them to think I told everyone in town but them."

"Fair enough," Paul said and offered a prayer before they left the house.

Angie led the way in her rusty Mustang with Kate following in her Honda. When they arrived, Angie pulled into the long driveway, and Kate parked her car in front of the brown split-level. She got out and met Angie at her car.

The girl was a nervous wreck. She twisted a piece of paper in her hands this way and that, and she kept sighing. They went to the front door, which Angie opened. Two of Angie's younger sisters—Angie introduced them as Amy and Kris—were playing a board game in the living room.

Angie said, "Where are Mom and Dad?"

"In the kitchen," Amy, who looked like a younger version of Angie, said. She watched them walk past—Kate could feel her stare—no doubt wondering what this stranger was doing in her house.

Mona and Ryan Petzel stopped talking when they came in.

"What's going on?" Angie's father asked, looking from his daughter to Kate.

"I'm Kate," she said, reaching to shake hands first with Ryan and then his wife. "Angie asked me to come along because she has something to tell you."

One of Angie's other sisters meandered into the kitchen. Angie turned to glance at her. Then she said, "Can we go talk somewhere else, like up in your bedroom?"

Mona and Ryan exchanged troubled looks. Kate felt for the couple, knowing the pain that was coming.

"Okay," Ryan said, rising from his chair and leading the way to the second-story bedroom that was neatly decorated in cornflower blues and tan and had a country feel.

Angie sat on the bed while Mona and Kate took the wing-backed chairs by the bay window that overlooked the back-yard. Ryan remained standing with his arms crossed over his chest. He shut the bedroom door.

"Mouse, is there something wrong?" Mona said, looking at her daughter. Kate smiled at the nickname.

"I've been wanting to tell you for a little while," Angie began. She closed her eyes, and Kate sent up a prayer for courage. "I've been so afraid of how you'd react. And I'm so sorry for disappointing you . . ."

"Angie?" Ryan drew closer to his daughter, and she lifted her face to his.

"Dad, Mom, I'm pregnant." She let out a staggered breath.

There was a long moment of silence. "You're *pregnant?*" Mona moaned.

"How could you have done this to us?" Ryan said, his words a hiss, and his face growing red. "You were raised better."

"I'm sorry, Dad."

"How long have *you* known?" he said to Kate with a hint of accusation in his tone.

"Angie told me about it Friday night," Kate said truthfully.

"How far along are you?" Mona said to Angie.

Ryan paced to the window, shaking his head.

Angie pulled her gaze from him to her mother. "Almost three months," she said.

"Three months," he repeated. "It's that Todd DeBoer kid, isn't it?" He turned to look at her.

Angie nodded mutely.

"I told you that boy was no good," he said to his wife. "We've been too lenient with her. We both knew that he was trouble. I can't believe you would do this, Angie. What kind of an example is this for your sisters?"

"I know, Dad."

"You *know*, you *know*!" he was practically shouting. "It's not just your sisters either. The kids at church look up to you. You've thrown it all in the trash." He turned to pace the room.

Mona dabbed her eyes with a tissue. "It's my fault," Mona moaned. "If I'd been home more, maybe I would've known what was going on with—"

"Is he going to marry you?" Ryan interrupted.

Angie shook her head. "He doesn't want to have anything to do with me or the baby."

"Isn't that just perfect? He gets my daughter pregnant, but it doesn't affect his life at all. He can just go his merry way."

Kate felt the man's pain.

"What about your future?" he went on. "You had a scholarship! What's to become of that?"

"Honey," Mona said, lifting teary eyes, "what are you going to do?"

"I don't know, Mom. I don't know."

Angie sighed, and he turned on her. "You think your
actions only affect yourself? They affect all of us, young lady.
Who do you think will end up raising your baby? Us? If it's
you, you can forget having a career. Everything you make at
that ice-cream parlor will go to buying diapers and baby food.
And it isn't fair to ask your mother to raise your child. After
all she does for you!"

"Ryan," Mona began.

"No, Mona. We're not taking away the consequences of
her choices. We just can't."

"But we can forgive her," she said.

Kate couldn't have been more thankful for Mona's words
of wisdom.

"This isn't about forgiveness. I haven't even begun to
think about forgiveness. I'm looking at this practically, Mona."

He turned back to Angie. "Do you know how selfish this
is of you?"

Angie nodded. "I do. If I could undo it, I would." Her
voice was small, sincere.

Her father's face relaxed a fraction.

"I just hope someday you'll be able to forgive me," Angie
said.

Mona looked over at Kate. "What do you think we should
do?"

The question was earnest, and Kate thought for a long
moment before answering.

"I know you're disappointed. I would be too if I were you.
And I know you love your daughter." She glanced at Angie,
whose eyes welled with silent tears. "I think that's where I

would start, just letting my daughter know that I still love her and that I'll help her figure out what to do."

Mona dabbed at her eyes, and Kate patted her hand.

"We do love you, Mouse," Mona said. "I know I've been busy with your sisters and church . . . I'm sorry you didn't feel you could tell us before." She moved to her daughter and held her.

"I'm sorry, Mom," Angie murmured. "I'm so sorry."

Ryan seemed glued to his spot, though he watched his wife and daughter. Kate knew he was struggling. Yet she hoped eventually he'd be able to forgive.

IT WASN'T EXACTLY a sense of joy or even relief that Kate felt when she left the Petzel home. The days ahead of the family would be difficult ones, but at least Angie had made that first critical step.

Kate kept thinking about the Lewises. She prayed she'd get a green light soon to tell Kim and Chad that there was a baby for them.

That night there was a message in Kate's in-box from Angie.

Dear Mrs. Hanlon,

I want to thank you for being there today. It was so hard. I can't imagine how I would've survived without you as my moral support.

We told my sisters. I hadn't thought that I had any more tears in me, but I was wrong. I feel like I really let them down; they look up to me. I told them I was sorry and that I want to be a good example. I only hope they can make better choices in their lives than I have. You've taught me that I can be forgiven. I'm so glad for that. It helps me to know that my life isn't over.

I asked my folks about adoption, but it's hard. Especially for Mom, knowing she'll never know her grandchild. But I've thought about adoption a lot, and I do think it's the best option.

Mouse

Chapter Twenty-Six

Kate, Paul, Chad, and Kim pushed their plates away and sat back in their seats. They'd decided to meet at the Bristol instead of at the Hanlons' for that night's session. The restaurant, on the first floor of the Hamilton Springs Hotel, was empty save for their table by the window that overlooked a pond, with the valley and rolling hills beyond. Kate desperately wanted to tell them about Angie. She just needed the right opportunity.

At their previous session, Paul had given the Lewises an assignment to go on an old-fashioned date, from Chad planning it ahead of time, with surprises for Kim throughout the night, to the kiss on the front porch at the end.

"So," Paul said, "how was your date?"

Kim smiled at her husband. "It was so romantic. Chad packed a picnic basket. We went to the park and ate, then he pulled out paper and paints, and we made a kite. It was so much fun." She grinned broadly.

"Did you fly it?" Kate asked.

"Of course," Chad said. "It was a pretty good kite if I do say so myself." He squeezed his wife around the shoulders. "I forgot how good it felt to date her."

"Making the effort to plan time together shows thoughtfulness and appreciation," Paul said simply. "Women eat it up."

They all laughed.

"So," Paul said, sitting back, "what else . . . ?" He looked from Kim to Chad.

Kim glanced nervously at her husband, then she said, "Well, we wanted to ask if you've found another couple to lead the youth group?"

"No," Kate said with a glance at Paul.

"Would you like to volunteer for the job?" Paul asked.

Chad smiled encouragement at his wife as she said, "We had an awesome time at the car wash, and we got to talking about it. It's not that I didn't enjoy working at the Faith Freezer Program, but our hearts are really with kids, you know?"

"We would love to have you take over for Max," Paul said. "Are you sure? It's a lot of work."

"Well, we can't make it a permanent position, considering the next tax season is right around the corner," Chad said, "but we will volunteer often. Then maybe someone else can take over when my workload gets hectic again."

Kim was smiling. "There is something else," she said, reaching for her husband's hand. She took a deep breath. "We've decided to adopt."

"We've been talking it over," Chad added, "and we think you're right. Maybe God wants us to go this route. I know it'd make Kim happy."

It'd make Kim happy. Kate paused at the comment, trying to decide what he meant by it.

But Kim picked the conversation up from there. "It'll make *both* of us happy. We still haven't given up on the idea of having biological kids. Maybe we'll be like the Andersons once we adopt." She turned to Kate. "I went on that Web site you told me about that had the pictures of the waiting children—toddlers and even teenagers. It about broke my heart. We'd want an infant, though."

"Actually," Kate began. "There is a girl I wanted to tell you about . . ."

Kim sat forward in her chair. "What do you mean?"

"She's been e-mailing me for the past few weeks. She's eighteen, unmarried, and pregnant."

"She wants to give us her baby?" Kim's tone rose in enthusiasm.

"That's what we want to talk to you about," Kate said. "She's a sweet girl, but she isn't ready to be a mother."

"Who is she?" Kim said. "Is she from Copper Mill?"

"She's a senior at Copper Mill High School. She's a very special girl, gifted in art and sewing. She has a scholarship to Parsons New School for Design in New York City. You should see the clothes she designs."

"She told you she wants to give her baby up?" Chad asked.

Kate nodded.

"How far along is she?" Kim asked.

"Almost three months. Her baby is due in October."

"Do you know anything about the father?" Chad asked.

"I don't know much about him other than he's in college and plays football . . . and he isn't interested in being a father.

But if you want to meet her, I'm pretty sure we could arrange that."

Kim turned to Chad, hope building in her eyes. "What do you think?"

"Six months is a long time to wait," he said.

"I'd venture that most adoptions take a lot longer," Kim said. "Besides it's not nearly as long as we've been waiting. And it's less than nine months . . ."

Chad smiled, reaching to squeeze his wife's hand. "Can you set up a meeting?"

Kate glanced at Chad. His expression wasn't nearly as enthusiastic as his wife's.

When the Lewises finally met with Angie the following Friday, she wouldn't look them in the eye, not at first, at least. Kate watched as Angie, her parents, the Lewises, and Paul sat together in the Hanlons' living room. Angie was next to her mother on the couch, holding her hand. She chewed her bottom lip and fidgeted with the hem of her blouse with her free hand.

"So, Kate tells us you want to study to be a fashion designer," Chad said, "and that you've been accepted at Parsons?"

Angie nodded. "That's always been a dream of mine."

"It's hard to get into that school, isn't it?" Kim said.

Angie shrugged. Kim glanced at Kate, the expression on her face clearly asking her to ease the awkwardness.

"Angie," Kate said. "Do you have questions for the Lewises? Or Mona, Ryan, do you have questions?"

"I read through your packet," Mona began, referring to

the information Kim and Chad had put together to tell them a bit about their home life. "You seem like a very nice couple. You share our faith, which is really important to us." She glanced at Ryan.

He sat with his arms crossed in front of him, his face twisted in sadness.

"This is all so difficult for us," Mona went on. "The thought of making an adoption plan for this baby . . ." She sighed, and tears came to her eyes. "I don't know." She looked over at Kate. "This is our grandchild."

"This is going to sound presumptuous," Kate said, "and that's not my intent, so take it with a grain of salt. But I feel this is the reason God placed both of you in my life at the same time. Because he's offering a solution for two very difficult situations. That's how God is, illuminating hope when it's hard to find."

"I know God does that," Mona said, "but the thought of not seeing this baby grow up . . ."

"We'd like an open adoption," Kim said. "We want you to know this child and to love him or her. After all, no child is a possession to hold on to tightly. We're only stewards for a little while. He or she would be better off knowing you, we feel."

Mona blew out her breath as tears rolled down her cheeks. "Really?" the word squeaked out.

"The truth is," Chad added, "we don't have a lot of family. Both Kim and I are only children. My parents are deceased, and Kim's are missionaries in Indonesia. We could use some grandparents for this baby, and an auntie." His gaze met Angie's.

An auntie. It struck Kate as a perfect solution.

Finally Angie held out a hand to shake with Kim and Chad.

"I want you to have this baby," she said. "You'll love it and take good care of it."

Kate glanced at Kim, whose face was wet with mascara smudges. She opened her mouth to speak, then she closed her eyes as emotion overwhelmed her. Her shoulders shook, and she sobbed while her husband held her hand.

Finally she managed, "I didn't think this day would ever come."

Chapter Twenty-Seven

K ate was putting on her lipstick when the doorbell rang the next morning. She opened the door to find Betty Anderson, with her bleached-blonde hair and dark roots, and Renee Lambert in a pink velour pantsuit and leopard-print hat. She looked like something out of a Dr. Seuss children's book.

Kate glanced questioningly at Betty, who said, "I hope you don't mind. I was telling Renee about making it up to you for Ronda's hair fiasco with our little prom-shopping excursion, and she wanted to come."

"Of course I don't mind," Kate said. "Where's Livvy?"

"We're going to pick her up at the library. She had something to finish up."

Kate grabbed her handbag and came outside, closing the door behind her. She could hear Kisses whimpering in Renee's designer tote.

"What's wrong with Kisses?" she asked.

"Oh, he doesn't want to go shopping," Renee said.

Kate exchanged a glance with Betty as she climbed into Betty's big green SUV. A dog who had an opinion on shopping? Kate couldn't resist. "What does he have against shopping?"

"He thinks I don't give him enough attention when we go. He's gotten so spoiled."

Betty started the vehicle, and they were off to get Livvy. Then the group set off for Chattanooga.

The drive was uneventful. It was a warm April day, no need for a coat. The women talked about the afterprom party and could scarcely believe it was coming up so soon.

By the time they reached Hamilton Place, the biggest and best mall in the area on the outskirts of Chattanooga, it was almost ten o'clock.

LuAnne rubbed her hands together. "Are we ready to hit the stores?" she said with a glint in her eyes.

"I don't know about you all, but I was born ready," Renee said. She patted Kisses' head and climbed out of the SUV.

The mall was fairly quiet, though there were always some shoppers even in the middle of the week. They made their way to Belk, by far the largest store in the mall, with its separate locations for women's and men's apparel, home decor, and kids' clothing and accessories.

Kate pulled out her list of needed prizes for the afterprom party and found a shopping cart. LuAnne and Betty each took one too, knowing that the gifts would fill the back of the big SUV. They made quick work of spending the money they'd earned at the car wash for the event and took the items to the SUV. Then they got lunch and left the mall, heading east of Signal Mountain in search of the Va-Va Vintage clothing store.

"The kids are going to eat this up," Livvy said.

She'd been pretty quiet all morning. Kate glanced at her and smiled.

"Did you tell James what we're doing?" she said.

"No. I want to surprise him. When he sees me in a tacky prom dress going out the door to the Grand March where all his friends will be . . ." She laughed.

"That will be priceless," Kate said. "Who is he taking to prom?"

"Anne. They're going as friends. Teenagers are amazingly resilient," Livvy said, shaking her head.

With plenty of shopping in downtown Chattanooga, the women cruised between stores. It was a perfect day for strolling. Betty pulled the vehicle to a stop on Hixson Pike, north of the Tennessee Riverpark, and killed the engine.

"This is going to be fun," Renee said, with a wink at Kate.

The women laughed at each other as they tried on dress after dress. Livvy put on an off-the-shoulder number with beaded sequins across the bodice and a skirt that fit a bit too snugly until it hit the knees, where it flared out in a big ruffle. It was a sea-foam color that complemented her auburn hair. She turned around in front of the mirror, looking at it from every angle.

"I look like a mermaid," she said. Then her eyes met Kate's as a smirk lit on her lips. "I think I'll take it."

Kate laughed so hard, she thought she'd cry. Then Renee came out in a very tame, for her, red dress. It had short capped sleeves and a square neckline with an empire waist. The fabric was light and airy and flowed gracefully when she moved. She turned her thin frame around as she looked at it in the mirror, then she shook her head and said, "Not this one."

Kate and Betty had already purchased their dresses. Kate's was a 1970s-era dress with patchwork-like fabric and platform shoes that added the perfect touch. Betty had gone for a fringed cowgirl-themed dress, with a hat and boots. She was still perusing the store, looking at racks and occasionally holding an item up for Kate to see.

Kate glanced at her watch. Knowing Renee, they'd be there another hour, and it was already closing in on three o'clock.

Livvy came back out with her mermaid dress draped over her arm and went to the checkout to pay for it.

Within a few minutes, Renee came out of the dressing room again. This time she sported a bright orange eyelet dress that was actually quite tasteful. She grinned at the mirror and fluttered a manicured hand to her chest.

"Now this is more like it," she said.

The hemline was a bit short for Kate's taste, but on Renee's skinny frame, it looked rather good.

"So, you're going to take it?" Kate said.

Renee nodded, keeping her gaze focused on herself. "I'll need to find a bag and shoes to match."

Kate smiled, thinking that would take another three hours.

Betty plopped into the padded chair alongside Kate and opened her shopping bag. "I found the cutest top for George's birth mom," she said, pulling out a pink ruffled blouse.

Just then, Kate's cell phone rang. She pulled it out of her

massive handbag and glanced at the display screen. It read *Kim Lewis.* Punching the Talk button, she said, "Kim, what's up?"

"Kate," the kindergarten teacher's frantic-sounding voice came over the line, "Chad's gone."

"What do you mean?"

"I don't have any idea where he is. I think he left me."

Chapter Twenty-Eight

When Kate arrived at the Lewises' home that evening, Kim was a panicked mess. Mascara smudges lined her cheeks and face all around her eyes, no doubt from an afternoon of crying.

"Come in," she said.

Kate had come as soon as Betty dropped her off at home to retrieve her car, and she'd told Paul what was going on.

Kim and Chad's two-story house was tan inside and out, with little in terms of style or decor. Kim plopped onto a yellow couch that reminded Kate of something she would've had in the 1970s, with its square, boxy look.

"How can he do this to me?" She looked as forlorn as a lost child. "Everything was going so well. How can he just walk away like that?"

"I'm sorry," Kate soothed. She placed an arm across the woman's back. She was shaking like a leaf.

"Did he leave a note or a message?" Kate asked.

Kim pointed to a wrinkled piece of paper on the coffee

table. She picked it up and read its contents again before handing it to Kate.

My dear Kim,

> *I'm sorry. When I saw that girl and how eager you were to adopt her baby . . . well, all I can say is, I didn't know what to think. I panicked.*
>
> *I love you. I really do. But I don't know if I'm ready to be a father. I want to be ready for your sake, for the baby's sake. But I don't feel ready. I guess what I'm saying is I'm scared. I know it's stupid of me to leave like this. But I need time to sort all this out. Time away from you and all the pressure I feel from Mr. and Mrs. Hanlon to be the perfect husband. To do all the things the church says I'm supposed to do.*

Kate paused, surprised. She hadn't meant to pressure the young man, though in retrospect she supposed she could understand why he might have felt that way.

> *I don't want to jump into this without being sure. Can you understand that? I know this will hurt you. And I'm sorry for that. I seem to be saying I'm sorry a lot. I don't know what will happen if I can't get past this.*
>
> *I guess we'll cross that bridge when we get to it.*
>
> *I need to find what I've lost. If I don't go back to the person I once was, I'm not sure I'll ever be the person I want to be.*
>
> *Chad*

Kate laid the letter back on the table.

"Do I look for him?" Kim lifted her tear-stained face to Kate. "Or do I take the chance that he'll never come back to me?"

Kate wasn't sure what to say. It was clear that Chad was confused and anxious. Had Paul been right that they weren't ready for adoption? And would tracking him down aggravate those frustrated emotions or dispel them? But when she looked at Kim and saw the agony in her eyes, she knew there was no choice.

"I know he's scared," Kim said, "and I know he feels a bit lost . . . but he wants a baby. He does. And I refuse to let our marriage fall apart because of fear. I want to find him, Kate."

KATE WAITED WHILE KIM put on a pot of coffee. Soon the smell of the rich Columbian brew reached their nostrils. Kate poured them each a cup, then they sat at the kitchen table, and Kate pulled a pencil and paper out of her handbag.

"I need you to think of where he might be," she said.

Kim shook her head. "I called his office and all of our friends. No one's seen him all day."

"What time did he leave the house?"

"This morning." Then she paused and took a breath. "He'd told me yesterday that he was taking garbage to the dump early. They had that computer trash day, where you can drop off stuff that can't just be tossed. He was going to take some of the PCs from the office down there."

Kate wrote as the young woman talked. "What time was that?"

"Eight o'clock?" She shrugged. "I'm not sure exactly."

"Did he say anything before he left?"

"We had breakfast—sausage and eggs. He actually seemed calmer than he'd been in a long time. I thought it was a good sign. I didn't know he was plotting to leave me! We were reminiscing about when we were dating that morning . . ."

Kate picked up the note and read it through again. "Where did you first fall in love?" she asked.

"Why do you ask?" Kim gave Kate a confused look.

"See this line—*If I don't go back to the person I once was, I'm not sure I'll ever be the person I want to be.* That's what he's searching for."

Kate held the note in front of each of them in turn. "If we can figure out what that means to him, I think we can find him."

"But I have no idea what he meant by that."

"What was he like in college?" Kate asked.

Kim paused to consider. "A lot of fun. Carefree. He got great grades, but he never needed to study. He loved life . . . and me." Tears returned, and Kim reached for another tissue from the box on the table.

Kate glanced at the oak surface, where several letters were strewn.

"What are those?" she asked.

Kim turned her head as she dabbed her eyes. "Oh, they're some old love letters Chad sent me in college." She shrugged. "I thought they might comfort me."

"Do you mind?" Kate said, motioning to the letters. "They might hold some clues."

"Help yourself."

Kate read several. There was nothing of much importance in them, at least not as far as finding out where he was. They were messages from a lovesick boy to the girl of his dreams.

Kim rubbed her eyes and looked at her watch. An hour had passed. She sent a text message to Chad.

"What did you say to him?" Kate asked, nodding toward the cell phone.

"Just that I love him and want him home."

"You didn't ask where he was?"

"No." She tossed the cell onto the table.

Kate glanced at the phone, and her eyes met Kim's.

"Don't search-and-rescue workers use cell-phone coordinates to find lost people?" Kim said.

"He's a grown man," Kate said. "It isn't like you can call search and rescue on him. He left of his own free will."

"True," Kim said. "But some cell phones have GPS capability. If he has it turned on . . ."

"But has he picked up at all today?" Kate asked.

Kim shook her head sadly. "It's gone to voice mail every time."

"Then it's probably not on," Kate said.

She reached for the last love letter from the pile and pulled out the unlined stationery. She'd come to recognize Chad's squared printing in the past hour.

My dear Kimmie,

I'm still reliving the glow of our day spent in Rock City.

Kate lifted her head as a thought came to her. "Didn't Chad mention Rock City in one of our counseling sessions?"

Kim nodded. "We used to go there all the time when we were in school. It's so pretty up there. We loved Deer Park and Swing-A-Long Bridge."

"What do you mean by 'all the time'?"

"Like every week, practically. He proposed to me on Lover's Leap."

Kate paused to consider the possibility that Chad had gone to Rock City. Wouldn't old memories have come crashing back there, breaking down his defenses? Yet he'd ignored Kim's many text messages. No, Kate decided, odds were he hadn't gone to the romantic spot. Kate had seen the way he'd looked at Kim during their counseling sessions, the love in his eyes. If he'd gone to Rock City he would've at least let Kim know he was okay.

There was another reason Chad had left—Kate felt it instinctively.

She said, "What is it that Chad really wants? Why do you think he left?"

Kim inhaled and thought for a moment. "He thinks he has to be perfect—the perfect husband, the perfect provider, the perfect father. That's why he drives himself so hard at work. And it's why not being able to have our own baby was such a big deal to him. Because not having a baby meant he was . . . a failure. Adopting means we *really* will be parents. It takes the whole idea out of the hypothetical and into reality. I think he's terrified that he'll put his all into being a dad only to fail at that too." She fidgeted with the centerpiece for a moment, then said in a soft voice, "He was adopted himself, you know."

"What?" Kate said. "Why didn't you tell us?"

"It's not something he talks about. You remember when he said that not all adoptions work out? He was talking about his own experiences. He's always had this idea that if he had stayed with his birth parents, things would've been easier, especially when his adoptive parents died in a car crash. He wouldn't have been an orphan at eighteen."

"Did he love his adoptive parents?"

"Deeply." Kim lifted her eyes. "That scares him too, I think. He's afraid of loving someone that much and losing them."

KIM ASKED KATE to stay with her that night. Kate called Paul at around nine thirty to let him know and he brought over a few supplies and prayed with them.

The young woman slept, though fitfully. Kate could hear her moving every few minutes through the paper-thin guest-room walls that night.

The following morning, Kate rose early. She had wanted some time alone in prayer to ask God what to do.

Lord, she began. *You are the great finder of the lost. Help us find Chad. Give Kim the wisdom and patience she needs to be the wife Chad longs for, the comfort he needs in his grieving.*

Kate hadn't thought of adoption as grief before, but she realized that a part of it had an element of grief. Birth parents grieved the inability to raise their own flesh and blood. Children grieved the unknown parents who gave them away. Adoptive parents grieved their inability to conceive. Some never recovered. Yet God understood grief all too well. He knew what it was like to lose a child, his own Son, and to lose humankind to sin.

Yet Kate also knew that adoption could bring healing to such wounds and give a family to a child without one. And it could offer fulfillment to couples who otherwise couldn't bear children. Best of all, Kate thought, the ultimate adoption brought humankind to a God who loved them.

At that thought, Kate lifted her face from her silent prayer. She knew where to find Chad—at least she had an idea. But she was going to need Kim's help.

Chapter Twenty-Nine

Kim hit the gas as they pulled onto the interstate heading toward Chattanooga that morning. The sun had just pushed over the horizon toward the blue sky.

"How do you know where to find him?" she asked Kate.

"I don't . . . exactly. But I do believe his leaving isn't just about your marriage. He said he had to sort things out, find who he was before. So I think it's about his adoption as much as finding the man he used to be when you dated. I have a couple places up my sleeve."

Kim glanced at her. Kate could tell she was considering what that meant.

"So, where would he go?"

"That's what we need to figure out. He's searching for any place where he feels connected to his family, his origins. Do you know where he grew up?"

"I've been there more times than I could count."

WHEN THEY REACHED CHATTANOOGA, Kim made her way to an older neighborhood of Southern-style homes. She pulled to a stop in front of a house with white columns and a wide porch and nodded toward it.

"This is where he grew up," she said. "He has never stopped talking about how much he loves the place."

Kate glanced at her watch. It was only eight thirty, but a man came out of the house just then. He wore running clothes and sneakers.

"Come on," Kate said.

"Can you help us?" Kim said, capturing the man's attention.

He was young, in his early thirties, Kate guessed, with dark hair and equally dark eyes.

"We're looking for someone who used to live here." Kim pulled a photograph out of her purse and handed it to the man. "Have you seen him?"

He studied the shot for just a moment, then nodded. "He was here yesterday, even asked for a tour."

"Did he say anything about where he was going?" Kate asked.

"Talked mostly about his family. They were killed in a car crash?"

Kim nodded.

"Anything else?" Kate asked.

"Not really."

They thanked him and turned to go. At least they were on the right trail, Kate thought. Now to their next stop.

When they got back in the car, Kim pulled her cell phone out of her purse. She studied the display for a long moment, clicking a few buttons to check her messages. She shook her head. Nothing from Chad.

Kim lifted her gaze and handed the cell to Kate.

"Can you type a text message for me?"

"Of course." Kate pulled up the text-message screen, and Kim dictated while she drove.

Chad, let me be there for you. Let me comfort you. Don't shut me out.

Then she hit Send.

When Kate looked around, she realized that Kim hadn't told her where they were going.

"He wants to be near family, his adoptive family. That's why he visited his old house . . . ," Kate said.

Kim nodded and met her gaze. "You're right," she said. "I think I know just where to look."

THE GRASS WAS COVERED in early morning dew. Sunlight eased through the trees, spotlighting particular headstones as they arched upward. Kim drove slowly along the narrow road that was the path through the graves, turning to the left until Chad's slender form came into view.

His back was to them, but there was no doubt it was Chad. His blond hair was tousled as if he'd come straight from bed.

"Do you want me to join you?" Kate asked Kim.

Kim nodded. "I need the moral support." She exhaled a heavy sigh, then added under her breath, "Thank God we found him."

She parked the SUV, and the two women got out. When they shut the doors, Chad turned toward them. He didn't move, didn't make any attempt to leave.

"How did you find me?" he said, when they reached him.

"I know you," Kim said simply. "I'm your best friend."

He smiled.

"I got your text messages. I'm sorry, Kimmie. I didn't want to hurt you."

"Please let me be your wife," she said. There was no accusation in her voice, just sadness. "I want to be here for you, Chad. Whatever you're going through, I want to go through it with you."

"I don't know if you can." He turned toward his adoptive parents' headstone. "They'd know what to tell me," he said.

There was a long silence. Finally Kim said, "They'd tell you not to be afraid."

Chad nodded.

"I have no idea what kind of a father I'd be."

"I do."

He met her gaze.

"Hopefully a better father than a husband, right?"

"No. You're a great husband. The best."

He smiled into her eyes. "I love you," he said.

"I love you too."

KATE DROVE KIM'S SUV back to Copper Mill while the Lewises followed in Chad's Mercedes. There was much to discuss when they got home.

Kate thought of Angie.

What would the girl do if Kim and Chad decided not to go ahead with the adoption? The idea of an open adoption had been the clincher for her. Would she be able to find another couple who wanted her to know her child, who wouldn't be threatened at her presence in their lives?

Kate loosened her grip on the steering wheel and decided not to worry about it. Instead, she lifted a prayer and let the beauty of the April morning calm her.

Chapter Thirty

Six days passed. Kate hadn't heard from Kim and Chad since dropping off Kim's SUV at the Lewises' home when they got back from Chattanooga on the twenty-seventh. She'd wanted to give them time, especially after Chad's comment about feeling pressured by her and Paul. She wouldn't have called if youth group hadn't been scheduled for the following day.

The phone rang three times before Kim finally answered, "Hello, Lewises."

"Kim, it's Kate. How are you?"

"Doing better, thanks."

"That's good to hear, Kim."

"Yeah. Chad and I are . . . working things out."

"Good." She paused. "I was actually calling about youth group tomorrow . . ."

"Oh, I meant to call you and tell you that we'll be there."

"Are you sure?"

"If you'll have us. We're still planning on chaperoning the afterprom party too."

"Of course. Kim, I don't know how to bring this up, but . . ."

"You're wondering about the baby?"

"Yes."

Kate heard her intake of air.

"We're working that out."

"Would it help Chad to talk to Betty and Bob again?"

"I doubt it." She grew quiet.

"If there's anything I can do, just let me know," Kate offered.

"Thanks," Kim said and then hung up.

THE NEXT DAY, as Kate and Paul were just sitting down to enjoy their Sunday lunch, a knock sounded on the door. Kate looked at Paul as he went to answer it.

She could hear Kim's and Chad's voices, so she joined them in the foyer.

"We want to adopt Angie's baby," Chad said.

"Wow, big news. Come tell us," Paul said, leading them into the kitchen. Kate pulled two more plates out of the cupboard for lunch.

"Don't go to any trouble," Kim said. "We didn't realize you'd still be eating." It was after two o'clock. "We were so excited we had to stop by."

"It's no trouble," Kate insisted. "There's plenty of pot roast in the oven." She finished setting their spots and filled two glasses with water.

"You didn't tell Angie that we were considering changing our minds, did you?" Chad asked Kate.

"No." Kate smiled. "I was hoping you'd come around."

Kim exhaled relief. "Good. We were afraid she might've talked to another couple."

"Will she be at youth group tonight?" Chad asked.

Kate had never seen him so excited.

"Yes. I talked to her yesterday."

"I'll call her too," Kim said. "We need to get to know her better."

"Can I ask," Paul leaned in, catching Chad's eye, "what changed your mind?"

Chad reached for his wife's hand and squeezed. "Kim asked me if I loved my folks. Despite everything, including teenage angst that I probably would've gone through adopted or not, and despite losing my parents at such a young age . . . I still wouldn't have changed a thing. They were the greatest parents. They loved me beyond words. Kim helped me see that I could love a child like that."

"Do you know your birth parents?" Kate asked, recalling Betty's mention of George's birth mother and that they were still friends.

"I looked for my mother but never had the courage to actually meet her."

"But our baby will know her mother," Kim said.

"Both of her mothers," Chad corrected.

WITH PROM QUICKLY APPROACHING, and the final details for the afterprom party to tie up, Kate was thrown into a melee of activity the following week.

She checked with each of the area leads to make sure everything was a go. She made arrangements for an extra cleaning of the church. With the event ending just hours before Sunday-morning church, they'd opted to skip Sunday school for the day. It was a sacrifice, but one the congregation willingly made.

Decorating commenced on Monday in the fellowship hall in the Faith Briar Church basement. The booths were already in their assigned spots. The men had run extension cords to the stations that would need electricity. The rented games came on Thursday in a large semi. The company spent the day checking and double-checking that everything was secure and running properly. Large fans added a constant hum to the fellowship hall.

Betty and Kate hauled in the vanload of prizes they'd purchased and took them to their assigned spots at each of the games. Kids would get awards for just attempting to play.

On Friday, the donated treats and bar cookies that had been promised by various members of the community started arriving in nine-by-thirteen inch pans. Renee checked each food item off her list and then wrapped the snacks in individual colored cling wrap for easy distribution and set them in the refrigerator for the following evening.

Even the photo booth, where the kids would pose for wacky pictures, was set up in a corner.

By Saturday morning, there was nothing left to do but wait for the fun to begin.

SINCE PROM ITSELF went until midnight, the festivities at the church didn't begin until late. Kate had taken a long nap that afternoon to be sure she'd be able to stay awake for the event.

She couldn't remember the last time she'd stayed up all night on purpose.

The grand march was at four o'clock. This was when the community gathered at the high school's auditorium to appreciate how fine their children looked all dolled up in fancy attire. Each couple took a stroll along the runway and were applauded for not tripping. Kate donned her 1970s prom dress, with its patchwork-effect fabric and platform shoes. She seemed to remember wearing something very similar to it when she was in college. If only she still had the long, straight hair to go with it. Instead, she opted to wear a tie-dyed headband across her forehead.

Paul came out of the bathroom wearing a pair of jeans and a button-down shirt. He paused to take in the full effect of Kate's outfit. "You're going out in public like that?" he asked.

"Livvy, Betty, Renee, LuAnne, and I all got . . . unique outfits for prom." She smiled. "The kids will get a kick out of them."

"All right, but I'm not wearing my gold lamé disco shirt."

"Why not?" Kate teased. "I was hoping you'd get out that old John Travolta outfit."

"You're very funny. Come on, we need to get to the high school."

THE SCHOOL'S GYMNASIUM was decorated in the Evening in Paris theme. A miniature replica of the Eiffel Tower with a backdrop of the city of love at one end of the gym served as the setting for photographs. A red-carpeted runway lit with lampposts served as the sole lighting. Parents and friends filled the stands, chatting among themselves. Kate and Paul made their way to a spot near the top where the Jenners were seated. Livvy wore her mermaid dress complete with sparkling green eye shadow.

"You're lucky you can pull off almost anything, Kate Hanlon, because that dress is hilarious," she said.

"Oh yeah? You're the one who looks like you should be selling tuna in a can."

Livvy laughed. "James was mortified that I was coming out in public like this. It was so precious. Poor guy."

The men looked at each other and rolled their eyes.

Betty and Bob Anderson came up the steps of the stands. Betty's cowgirl getup was a bit tight, but that only seemed to add to the tacky effect. People turned their heads to stare as she and her husband passed.

"Hey, hey," she said as she climbed the stands. Paul scooted over, making room for her to sit next to Kate. Bob went to sit with the men on the far side of the row. "He's embarrassed to be seen with me!" Betty said, giggling. Her makeup was particularly heavy.

When Kate studied Betty's eyes, she realized she was wearing fake eyelashes that looked like caterpillars climbing across her eyelids.

"Did I miss anything?" Betty looked around the gymnasium.

"No," Kate said. "Not really."

Just then, a young man tapped Betty on the shoulder, and she turned to see who it was. Kate assumed that her ten-gallon cowboy hat was blocking his view, and he was going to ask her to take it off. Instead, he handed her a note.

"What's this?" she said.

"That gentleman in the back sent it to you," he said, then hopped down to the gym floor.

Kate turned with Betty to see who he'd meant. She studied the faces, but everyone seemed focused on the festivities about to begin.

"What does it say?" Kate pointed to the note.

"Is it the same writing as your secret admirer's?" Livvy chimed in.

Betty looked at the outside, before tearing it open. She pulled out the flowery card that read, "Can I have this dance?" It was signed "Your secret admirer."

Kate didn't miss her quick glance to Bob. But he was immersed in conversation with Paul and Danny.

"The boy said he's here," Kate reminded.

Betty stood up and turned to get a better look. Finally she gasped. "Oh, I can't believe it!"

She sounded as if she was going to cry, and she covered her mouth with a bejeweled hand.

A twentysomething, good-looking man made his way toward her. He had a head full of dark, thick hair and pale blue eyes. With a chiseled face and a trim physique, he could easily have been a model. He wore a tuxedo and held a single rose in his hand.

"My goodness," Kate heard Livvy say.

Kate leaned to whisper to her, "Who is it?"

"It's her son, George."

By then, Betty was bawling. She held out her arms, and her tall boy gave her a huge bear hug.

"Oh, don't cry, Ma," he said.

"You look so handsome," she said.

Bob must have noticed what was going on because he too was on his feet and in line to embrace his son.

"Were you in on this?" Betty asked.

Bob shook his head. "I had no idea."

"When did you get in?"

"Half an hour ago. Thought I'd surprise you for Mother's Day tomorrow."

"Mission accomplished!"

"Did you like the flowers?"

Betty playfully slugged his arm. "Half of Copper Mill thinks I've been unfaithful!"

George blushed. "That wasn't my intent. I guess I forgot that small towns can be that way."

It was time for the grand march to begin. George took the seat next to the aisle. Betty held his hand. The principal came out and recognized the organizers of the event, including prom servers Marlee and Brenna, who wore beautiful gowns. Then the grand march commenced.

There was something magical about seeing the kids all dolled up and looking glamorous for the event. Many of the girls had their hair in updos, with curls strategically placed and ringlets framing their pretty faces. And the boys with their tuxedos and suits had become striking young men.

When Angie came out with her date, Kate was struck with how lovely the senior was. She wore a strapless dress in a pale salmon color, with delicate embroidery that trailed across the front and around the back like a drooping bouquet. It had an empire waist, so it was loose fitting across the stomach to hide her growing secret. Her hairstyle was simple, straight and shiny. Her date was shorter than she and wore a white suit.

Livvy leaned over to Kate and asked, "Who's her date?"

"That's Michael Bradley. He's a sophomore and her childhood friend."

The couple looked stunning together. When they paused at the end of the makeshift runway, Angie's gaze caught Kate's. She smiled, and Kate knew in that moment the girl was going to be just fine. God had his protective hand on her and on her child.

SINCE KATE WAS ALL DRESSED UP, Paul took her to dinner during prom, though when the waiter at the Bristol took in her retro outfit, she saw Paul's face turn five shades of red.

At around eleven, they headed to the church to wait for the afterprom party to begin. The scent of Tony's Pizza filled the fellowship hall as volunteers chatted and finished any last-minute preparations.

At midnight, an avalanche of teenagers descended on the church. Some still wore their promwear, but most had changed into more casual clothing that seemed out of place with their elegant hairdos. The rented photo booth and games were huge hits with the partygoers.

Kate manned the food table, handing out punch and making sure the table was well stocked for the ravenous crowd.

When Ronda came by to take her place in the booth, Kate noted how much healthier the young woman looked than the last time Kate had seen her. She was working the dart game next to Kate's table.

"You look like a new person," Kate said when there was a lull in the action.

"Thanks," Ronda smiled. "I feel like a new person now that I know what's wrong with me."

"What do you mean?"

"Turns out I really am allergic to perm solution. My doctor has me on some meds that are supposed to get my allergies under control."

"That's great," Kate said, noting that Angie Petzel had just arrived. She'd changed into jeans and a Copper Mill High sweatshirt in red and white.

"I was hoping to get another glimpse of Angie's dress," Ronda said, following Kate's gaze. "Did you see it? She made it herself. Didn't even use a pattern—how amazing is that? She's going to do really well when she gets to design school in New York."

Kate nodded her agreement.

Kim Lewis waved to her from her spot by the Velcro jumping wall. A boy ran past, jumping hard on the rebounder and gluing himself upside down to the wall. His friends squealed in delight, and Kim grinned as she went with Chad to peel his orange jumpsuit off the thing.

Ashley Williams was working the beanbag toss, bending to pick up the thrown bags and handing them to the next person in line. She came by Kate's table at around one thirty.

"I wish we'd had this when I was in high school," she said. She took a sip of her punch. "I needed this."

"How are you feeling?" Kate asked.

"Good." She smiled. Her gaze shifted to Carl Wilson, who was passing out basketballs at the free-throw game.

"Did you know Carl has a brother?" she said.

"I did," Kate said. "Jack."

"He's cute." She lifted her eyebrows. "I hadn't known they were brothers . . ."

Kate smiled inwardly, glad that the girl had started to move on.

"I better get back." She ambled to the beanbag toss and took up her spot once again.

Kate glanced around and realized that Angie and Kim were standing next to her. The expression on Kim's face said something was up.

"I was wondering when you'd make your way here," Kate said to Angie. "I loved your dress, by the way."

"Thanks." Angie gave her a long hug.

When she pulled back, Kate said, "So, what's going on with you two?"

Kim and Angie exchanged conspiratorial glances.

Angie said, "I have a favor to ask you, Mrs. Hanlon. I already asked Kim."

"Anything," Kate said.

"I've been thinking about it. Of course, my mom will be there, and I thought about maybe one of my sisters, but they aren't really the ones I want . . ."

Kate had no idea what she was talking about. Kim's smile grew.

"Well," Angie went on, "I could use a couple of birthing coaches."

Kate was stunned. She looked at Kim, who was nodding. "There are no two people I'd like to have there more than both of you," she said.

Kate placed a hand on her chest at the sudden emotion that came over her. Tears coursed Kim's cheeks.

"I'd love to," she said.

"Oh, I'm so glad," Kim said.

Angie smiled at both of them. "I told you she'd want to be there."

Epilogue

K ate and Paul were there at graduation. They saw Angie
receive her diploma. Kate's pride in the girl had swelled
when she took the stage and shook the principal's hand. She
had seen so much courage and determination in Angie during those months that she knew the girl would be more than
all right when all of this was over. Even though some in town
talked about her behind her back, Angie had held her head
high, confident that God had forgiven her and was giving her
a new future.

Summer had bloomed. Kate stopped often at Emma's to
see the young woman. Kate was happy that Angie continued
to report her father's growing level of acceptance of things as
they were. Her belly grew from a small bump to a large vol-
leyball, but she always looked adorable in the maternity cre-
ations she made for herself.

Kim and Chad had gone to every prenatal visit, asking
questions of the doctor and holding Angie's hand. So far, the
pregnancy had been smooth sailing. Angie had taken good
care of herself, and it showed.

Kate, Kim, Mona, and Angie had attended birthing classes in Pine Ridge together, practicing the breathing techniques for each phase of delivery. Kate had answered Angie's questions, though it had been a very long time since she'd experienced childbirth for herself.

Then autumn arrived in all its fickle bluster. Leaves fell from the trees, and most of Angie's classmates went off to distant colleges. Angie, Kate, and Kim had decided to take walks in the mornings before the birth, even when it was chilly.

They were headed up Sweetwater Street on a cold October day when Angie's water broke.

"Ohhh," she squealed.

Kate looked at her, not comprehending what was happening at first. Then she saw the puddle of liquid at the girl's feet.

Kim seemed the most surprised.

"What?" she said. "Are you okay?"

Angie squealed again. "My water broke." She pointed at the ground.

"Oh, oh, oh," Kim said, looking around.

A passerby on the sidewalk glanced at her as if she were having an episode, then he made his way into the newspaper office.

They took a few more steps.

"Should I call an ambulance?" Kim reached for the cell phone that was in her pocket.

"I don't think we need an ambulance," Kate said, enjoying Kim's excitement. "We're closest to your place. Let's go there."

It was only a block to the tan two-story home. They moved as quickly as they could, but Angie had to stop after half a block.

"Ouch," she said.

"What is it?" Kim said.

"I think . . ." She paused and placed a hand on her large, round belly. "It hurts so bad."

"You're having contractions," Kate said.

"Ugh," She looked at Kim and said, "This is going to be way more painful than I thought."

They made it the rest of the way to Kim's house without any more contractions hitting. Since it was Saturday, Chad was home tinkering in the garage. Kim called for him from the front entry, and he came in wiping his hands on a shop towel.

"What's going on?" he said, then his gaze moved to Angie, whose face had gone ashen. "Is she okay?"

"She's in labor." Kate took over. "Kim, get the car. Chad, call Angie's folks and let them know we're heading to the hospital. I'll call the hospital to let them know we're on our way." She glanced at Angie. "And please get a chair for her."

"And a towel," Angie called to Chad.

He returned a few minutes later with a wooden dining-room chair and a thick beach towel that he laid down for her to sit on. Kate dialed the hospital.

Within ten minutes, they were on their way to Pine Ridge.

"Your parents didn't answer the phone," Chad said to Angie.

She glanced at Kate with a look of panic in her eyes.

"We'll find them," Kate assured her. She reached for the eighteen-year-old's hand. Then she called Paul to tell him what was going on and to ask him to find Mona and Ryan.

They reached the hospital in less than fifteen minutes; Kate wondered how fast Chad was driving. The emergency-room staff was at the ready with a wheelchair to take Angie straight to labor and delivery.

Chad kissed Kim good-bye.

"I'll come out and keep you posted, okay?" she said.

Kate knew he was disappointed at not being able to be in the delivery room, but Angie hadn't been comfortable with the idea. He moved to one of the padded chairs and lifted his face to the TV in the corner.

Kate and Kim followed the fast-moving nurse through the corridors of the small hospital and into the labor-and-delivery wing at the end. Angie was transferred to a bed, and the nurse hooked up a heart monitor to check the baby's beats and a blood pressure cuff to keep track of Angie's pressure.

Contractions were a mere four minutes apart, and Kate knew that they had grown in intensity because Angie had stopped talking once they got to the hospital. Her eyes spoke of pain. Kim was at her side the whole time, watching carefully, concerned.

Kate's cell phone rang, and the nurse gave her a dirty look. She moved into the hall to take the call since it was from Paul.

"Angie's folks are at their church in Pine Ridge," he said. "They should be there any minute."

Relief flooded Kate.

"Thank you! I'll keep you posted on progress here."

"I'm already on my way," he said.

"YOUR FOLKS ARE ON THEIR WAY," Kate informed Angie when she came back into the room. The girl smiled. Then another contraction hit. Her face glowed with perspiration, and her eyes were fixed on Kim, as if she wanted the kindergarten teacher to know this moment deeply so she could share it later with their child. The sight was so achingly beautiful that Kate found herself choking up.

"It's almost time to push," the doctor informed.

"But my mom isn't here," Angie said, panic in her voice.

"Yes, I am," Mona said from the doorway. "Your dad's in the waiting room with Chad and Paul."

The nurse showed her where to scrub up and robe as she had done with Kate and Kim earlier.

Mona was back at her daughter's side by the next push.

Finally a beautiful baby girl emerged. Her face was pink and pinched, and her eyes were dark and seemed too large for her tiny face. She was squealing at the top of her lungs, and everyone in the room, including the medical personnel, laughed.

The nurse went to clean her off, and the doctor said, "You've got a boisterous one, that's for sure."

He was looking at Angie, and Kate felt a twinge of sadness for Kim.

But Angie said, "Yes, she does," her eyes on her friend.

Kate excused herself to get the men, and when she, Paul, Ryan, and Chad returned, the nurse was just bringing the baby back, bundled in a cotton hospital blanket.

"Who would like to hold her first?"

She began to hand the baby to Angie, but Mona said, "Her mother should hold her first," motioning toward Kim.

Tears streamed down Kim's cheeks as she took her daughter into her arms with Chad looking on at her side. The baby ceased her wailing, and Kim kissed her cheek.

There wasn't a dry eye in the room. Kate pulled several tissues out of the box on the bedside table and handed one to Mona and Angie before offering one to Kim.

"She's amazing," Kim said to Angie.

"I'm so happy for you," Angie said.

Kim smiled and placed the baby in Angie's arms.

"She's a gift to both of us," Kim said. "A miracle to fill our open arms."

About the Author

BEFORE LAUNCHING her writing career, Traci DePree worked as a fiction editor for many of the best Christian authors in the country. While still maintaining her editing career, Traci loves creating new worlds in her novels. Her hope is that, just as in Copper Mill, Tennessee, her readers will see God's creation and inspiration within the people in their own lives. Traci is the author of the best-selling Lake Emily series, including *A Can of Peas, Dandelions in a Jelly Jar* and *Aprons on a Clothesline*. She makes her home in a small Minnesota town with her husband and their five children, the youngest via adoption.

A Note from the Editors

THIS ORIGINAL BOOK was created by the Books and Inspirational Media Division of Guideposts, the world's leading inspirational publisher. Founded in 1945 by Dr. Norman Vincent Peale and Ruth Stafford Peale, Guideposts helps people from all walks of life achieve their maximum personal and spiritual potential. Guideposts is committed to communicating positive, faith-filled principles for people everywhere to use in successful daily living.

Our publications include award-winning magazines such as *Guideposts* and *Angels on Earth*, best-selling books, and outreach services that demonstrate what can happen when faith and positive thinking are applied in day-to-day life.

For more information, visit us at www.guideposts.com, call (800) 431-2344 or write Guideposts, PO Box 5815, Harlan, Iowa 51593.